Horror's Call

Call of the
Crocodile

by

F. Gardner

Chapter 1: Child's Play

Leaning against the wall, a young man wearing a visor grasps his gun, and peers down a dimly lit corridor. His green eyes move side to side, investigating the labyrinth, by what little light remained within it. "Looks like the coast is clear" he whispers to himself. Speedily, he lunges forward and embarks down the hallway. "No sign of danger, so far," the boy thinks as his eyes squint. It's nearly pitch black, but his glowing riffle and the dim neon lights on the wall illuminate the hallway.

"I think there's just a few minutes left," the young man muttered, as his head shuffles surveying the darkness. "What was that?" the question whispers through his lips as a large monstrosity emerges from the depths of the shadows. The figure lifts enormous scaled claws and lets out a ferocious roar. The boy's heart skips a beat, as he ready's his aim. With his rifle positioned at his target, while closing one eye, the young man pulls it's trigger, and blasts his reptilian adversary square in its beastly maw.

The lights in the room flash in unison with a booming alarm. Looking upward, the boy lifts his head toward a large television screen the size of a truck. "Winner: Pete" the words on the screen read. The young man takes a visor off of his head, and smiles. "Nice going, kid. Looks like you got the high score," remarks a gruff voice. "Exit's, this way. Enjoy your time here" the authoritative voice commands.

Like the radiant morning sun, the formerly dim room's lights switch on, as a man waves his hand, signaling several children to a door. Scattered about, the kids begin to form a line, and gradually exit the facility. "Thanks for playing. You kids all have a good day, now" the man says, as he directs them out. One by one, the children leave the room, as their gleeful chatter fills the bright autumn afternoon. "I think this game here is my favorite" the boy with green eyes tells the man, as he approaches the exit.

"That was a cool game, Dad. It seemed so real" the boy remarks, with the pupils of his green eyes constricting as he steps out of the door, into the light of the day. "I'm glad you're having a good time so far, Pete. I sure know I am" Joe his father remarks as Pete's toothy grin widens.

"Are you sure you don't want to change out of your costume? Rafe and Jimmy went to the room to change out of theirs" Joe asks. Pete was wearing an outfit which was as green as his eyes. "No, I'm not worried about that. Halloween's the only day you can pretend to be someone else, right? So, I should enjoy it while it lasts" the boy replies.

"Ha. You always have been an interesting kid. Most children your age probably wouldn't want to go trick or treating as a character that shares their

2

first name," Joe says to his son. "Nope. It doesn't bother me," the child confidently reassures his father. "Good. You have wisdom beyond your years," Joe says, delighted.

"You should try the game I just finished too, Dad" the boy stated to his father. "Ha, well I don't know. I think I'm a little too old for that sort of thing, don't you think?" the man says, while affectionately patting his son on the back. "Too old?" Pete inquires, tilting his head. "No way. You're never too old for fun and games" the boy, says shaking his head left to right in disapproval. "It doesn't matter how old you are. As long as you're having fun, you should do whatever you want to do," he tells his father. "Maybe, so" Joe says with a chuckle.

"Besides, you still like to play with Rafe, Jimmy and me, right? You do that all the time. You're not too old for that anymore, are you?" Pete says, continuing his rebuttal. "Fair enough. That's a good point, Pete" Joe responds to his son's refutation, as the chatter of the surrounding children began to die out.

The rest of the kids, all greet their respective parents, and go about their own paths. "Nice to see all these families here together, having a good time" Joe says, as the sight of the innocent children joyfully talking amongst their parents and siblings tug at his heartstrings.

"This was a good idea, Dad. Coming here on Halloween, that is" Pete says with conviction. "You think so? I'm glad you feel that way. I was a little worried it might turn out to be a bad idea. That it would be disappointing doing something so unusual. Considering it's on a holiday you boys all like so much" Joe tells him. "No, not at all. When you first suggested the idea, I was a little bit surprised. But I'm having fun," Pete responds.

"Great. It's good to change things up a bit, every once and a while. Don't you think so? It can get a little boring, otherwise. If everybody in the world, always just did the exact same thing, it could become tiresome. Year after year, never doing anything different. I think your brother's are having a good time, too."

"Yeah, I think it's really cool, too. Rafe and Jimmy, usually like amusement parks. This one's so unique, so they're probably having loads of fun" Pete says, as his view becomes fixated on a sign. "Live Exotic Animals, This Way" the sign reads, as Pete's green eyes gaze at it from the distance.

Walking through the amusement park, the duo is mesmerized by the magnificent architecture. "What an eclectic design. Old gothic statues, and colorful playsets for children. This theme park really sets the bar high. To think it's a resort, as well. I can't think of any other place that even compares to the scope of this place" Joe remarks.

"This sure is an interesting place isn't it, Pete? A resort with a playground, and even a zoo. To think this place used to be a church of some kind. It even still has some old church statues inside near the auditorium area" Joe says to his son. "I think that's kind of nice. Like having angels watching over us. What was that real big statue? The one above us while we were watching the show they had on the stage?" Pete asks. "It looked like some kind of an angel. Probably St. Michael" Joe, answers his son, as the two continue their leisurely walk through the captivating amusement park.

"So, if this place used to be a church. What's with all the creepy ads for it, on TV?" Pete asks, looking up at his father. "I think that's probably just marketing, since it's Halloween," Joe responds. "Hold on. Excuse me? One beer, please" Joe says to a man as they near a concession booth.

Paying for the beverage, Joe cracks open the aluminum can, and takes a sip. He burps loudly, which makes Pete giggle in amusement. "Dad, you know you're supposed to say excuse me" he says to his father, laughing. "You're right. Excuse me," Joe says, as he quickly finishes the drink, eager to resume their stay at the facility. "Nice, shot," Pete remarks, as his father tosses the empty can with ease, into a recycling bin, in the distance. "Thanks. Maybe I should've become a basketball player."

Noticing his son looking back in the distance,

Joe wondered what Pete was pondering, as it seemed the young man had something on his mind. "Something eating you, son? You look deep in thought" Joe inquires. "Can I look around on my own for a while?" Pete asks. His father, contemplates momentarily. "Well, I don't think you should go off on your own. Can't you wait just a little while longer for your brothers? I don't know what's taking them so long, but they should be getting back from our room, pretty soon," He asks as his son looks down in a sullen fashion.

Like a dog begging it's master for a treat, Pete's green eyes widen with impatience. "Come on Dad, I'm not that little, anymore. It's not like I can't ever go off on my own, like some baby. Besides, Rafe and Jimmy should be here any second," the young man pleads. "Alright, alright. I'll send your brothers over to you, when I see them" Joe, his father says, giving in to his son's protest. The young man excitedly trails off as he walks onward, in solitude.

Chapter 2: Dawn

Dreams are nothing more than a series of images projected by the subconscious. Joe had known that. The human mind strings the dreamt visions together in a narrative, even if the images don't necessarily go together. That's simply how our minds operate. Like a child playing a game of Ad-Libs, trying his or her best to make sense out of the hand they've been dealt.

Figments, which seem like phantoms in the night. But they're merely phantasms. Figment's of one's imagination. Like an hallucination brought on as the results of inebriation. Like the child's play of some kid's fabrication.

Joe had understood that, as he was not a superstitious man. But why did this feel like more than a mere dream? Almost more real than his waking moments. Do animals dream the same? Sequentially? Joe did not know. However, he felt as if he were now fated to find out, whether he wanted to or not.

More than that, Joe was beginning to feel like Sisyphus. The character found in Greek mythology. The one who had been condemned to eternally push a boulder up hill, only to have it roll back down repeatedly. As if he were in Tartarus. The Greek term for the abyss. It had begun to feel all too familiar. Too real for a dream.

It's a dream he's had many nights before. Several nights, all throughout the past year. Even though, Joe realized that this was just his imagination, it still felt to him as if he were revisiting the same horrific occurrence over and over.

"I might as well eat my own tail, since I have one in these dreams" Joe thinks to himself. It certainly felt like eternity. Especially considering that these simple minded creatures have no conception of time, and the more Joe found himself in these dreams, where he possessed a scaled body, the more he found himself losing his humanity and thinking like one of them. In his dream, Joe looked over toward his hands. At least, what should be hands. They were now, merely scaled appendages which bared little semblance to his waking form.

"No, don't do it" Joe thinks, as he sees a hand lift a gate to an unlocked position. Who's hand was that? Was it the hand of fate, at play? He didn't know. He did, however, know what was coming, as a foreboding sense of doom flowed through his mind.

Creeping and crawling past a gate which should be locked, he moves into a courtyard littered with children playing. Yes, Joe's human, in reality. But in these dreams, it's like primal instinct takes over him. As if he really were a beast now, and he could not control his actions. Animal's can do no real wrong.

8

They have no sense of morality. They only stalk, kill and consume their prey for survival purposes. But still, it felt wrong to Joe. Natural instinct clouds his judgement, as he approaches his own flesh and blood, as anxiety overwhelms him.

It's hard to imagine such a creature would pose a threat to anyone. Yes, these beasts have many teeth, all of them razor sharp. But the slow lumbering way they crawl, makes them easy to outrun. Of course, that is unless it's target were a defenseless child.

"There's no way I can watch this again" Joe thinks to himself with what paltry human cognition he had left. Arduously, he attempts to look away from what he's about to do. Joe bends his leathery neck, or what constitutes what passes for a neck in the corporeal form he's in. Lifting his head, he gazes at the deep azure sky.

Above him, he could see a pair of eyes gazing back at him. The eyes appear to be just as equally surprised to see him. "I have seen this being before, in my dream. Who is it? What is it? I don't know who it is. Maybe it's not for man to understand. Certainly not for a reptile. I'm inches away from my prey now, and my mouth salivates. These creatures are insatiable. Don't they ever get tired of eating?" The thoughts race through Joe's agonized mind.

"No! No, I can't watch this again! Even if it's just a dream" Joe screams to himself, as the gory meal takes place, once more. Blood drips from out of his fanged mouth, as tears flow down his face, onto the remains of the bloodied corpse. Although these creatures can't really cry. Not in the sense humans do. "It's just a dream," he continues to tell himself, trying to console his guilty conscience.

At last, Joe's eyes open as the man awakens in his bed. The first thing he hears upon waking was the ticking of the grandfather clock in the room. Relieved the nightmare was over, Joe attempts to calm his heart-rate by breathing slowly. The sweat drips down his forehead in unison with the infernal ticking.

The word resonates within the man, as Joe reflects on the matter. About how it aptly describes his feelings. Infernal. As in the word "Inferno" The chapter from Dante's Divine Comedy. If the rest of his life is anything like that story, he can only hope that the subsequent chapters sync up as well. Purgatorio and then finally Paradiso. Purgatory and Paradise. Joe and his family, whole once more. Together, in elysian peace. The man begins to calm down, feeling he has grasped a glimmer of solace.

He tries not to become discouraged, but is indeed developing an inkling that a happy outcome, may be less of an eventuality, and more of a delusional fantasy. Joe fears that despite whatever valor resides within him, his desires of an absolution and tranquility are as fake and insincere as crocodile tears. Fears that his chances of mending his faux pas will go unheeded.

"This has gone on long enough" thought Joe. "I have to get ready to start my day." The man looks out of his window, and glances at the morning sun. The sun, was in the midst of rising. Joe can take solace knowing that nightmares will haunt him no more. At least not till the next night. For the day had officially begun. Things had begun innocently enough, as they usually tend to during this time of year.

A cool breeze, blows the bright orange and crimson leaves across the street as they tempestuously gather together forming a vibrant hodgepodge near the sidewalks. Children use the colorful assortment of leaves to play in and adults used rakes and leaf blowers to clear off their lawns. Summer was long gone, and the season of autumn had engulfed the town. Consumed unconditionally, just as Jonah had felt entrapped in the belly of the great fish. Jack O' Lanterns and similar traditional décor of the season enveloped the land.

Chapter 3: Trepidation

Sitting in an office room of modest size, Joe finds himself with an appointment with his doctor. His psychiatrist Dr. Boltzmann, remains composed with a notepad, while Joe rests on a couch. In a state of unease, the disheveled looking man, clears his throat and begins to discuss his plight. "Feels like I'm in Hell" Joe says. "What was that?" his doctor asks. "I said, it feels like I'm in Hell" Joe repeated blankly. "Or at least Purgatory" he continued.

"Do you believe in Hell?" Joe asks of his physician. "I'm not sure if I do, Joe. I try not to dwell too much worrying about the conditions of the hereafter. The reputable hereafter, that is" the doctor answers, scribbling away in his notepad. "I see. I guess it seems you're at the very least, a skeptic" Joe, inquires. "How can I not be? I specialize in the field of medicine, and the study of the mind."

"My chosen career, naturally makes me question things. It tends to be invariable in my profession. Or at least, to an extent" Dr. Boltzmann says. "Chosen? So, you don't believe in fate at all? You mean like what men of the cloth refer to as a calling?" Joe asks. "I wouldn't say I necessarily do. If I did though, I'm not certain it's relevant. If I'm to be entirely honest with you."

"As much as I enjoy discussing philosophical matters with you, I'm afraid I'm going to have to change the subject. I wouldn't want you to feel cheated out of the money you're paying me by just discussing my personal beliefs. We're here right now to talk about you. To discuss your problems" Dr. Boltzmann says. "I understand. Sorry."

"No, don't be sorry, it's alright. Now, what happened to your hand?" The doctor asks. "Oh, it's nothing" remarks Joe, as he casually puts his hand into his pocket. "I see. Well, it's been about a year since your son died, correct?" Asked Dr. Boltzmann. "One year tomorrow, yes," Joe answers, as he restlessly repositions himself on the leather couch.

"To think it happened on a vacation. While we were at a resort. A very unusual resort. Since, it has an amusement park in the middle of it. But still a resort all the same. At what I considered to be such a safe area of it too, of all places. It was supposed to be a happy time for us all. A relaxing place to unwind, and have a good time. Instead it was the worst experience of our lives" Joe says, glumly.

"What occurred, was unthinkable. I mean, the very notion of the matter, is quite literally anathema. Do you know that term? It's a word meant to describe Hell. The absolute, unconditional, suffering of the place. It means...a fate so terrible, it would be better to have never been born. Can you imagine that?" Joe asks in exasperation.

The doctor shakes his head. "No, I can't say I can, Joe. I imagine that it's indeed as you describe.

13

Unthinkable. A thought too grim, to virtually all parents."

Yes, it did feel like Hell. There was no doubt about that to Joe. As the poet Delmore Schwartz famously coined- "Time is the fire in which we burn." Every moment in time, ticked away at Joe's life. He felt as if he were preforming some sort of meta-physical form of mortification of the flesh. Self-Flagellation. Like how a pious monk would whip himself with his belt in order to obtain indulgences. Time off his sentence from Purgatory. It had sounded nice albeit morbid, but it was simply unrealistic. Too wishful for a man like Joe to desire. The futility of these thoughts tempted him to ask for his doctors insight.

Although his thoughts were figurative, Joe felt he had better hold his tongue, and not mention it to the doctor. As poetic as he thought his day-dreams to be, Dr. Boltzmann was a psychiatrist. A man of science. "I don't want him to inadvertently get the wrong impression, and really think I'm crazy" Joe thought. He had realized the irony of his thoughts, as he was seeing the doctor for his own mental health. Joe, silenced his contemplation, and lent his doctor his ears. Fidgeting in his seat, and adjusting his posture, Joe proceeded to give the doctor his undivided attention.

"How about your dreams, Joe?" Dr. Boltzmann asks. "My dreams? I'm afraid you'll have to be a little more specific than that, doctor. I have dreams, well nightmares all the time" Joe replied. "Yes, I know. What about that one where you're in a forest? You've mentioned that one to me a few times" inquired the doctor.

Scratching his chin, Joe contemplated the subject. "Well you see, I haven't actually had that one for a while. But, that's true. I do tend to have that one fairly frequently. Certainly more so, than the majority of the other reoccurring dreams I happen to have. I wonder why I haven't dreamt that recently" Joe responded, leaning his head to his side, in vexation.

"That one doesn't sound too bad. Your forest dream, that is. You just go into a treehouse of some sort, right? You sure it's just not an old childhood memory you're dreaming about? Dreaming that you're playing in your backyard, when you were a kid?" Dr. Boltzmann asks, leaning in closer, with curiosity.

"A childhood memory? No. I don't think so. You see doctor, my mother still owns the house I grew up in. So, I'm fairly confident that I'd remember if we had a treehouse or not. Besides, it's not so much what happens in the dream, but rather the feeling I get. Whenever I have that dream, I start to get a sensation that I've been there before" Joe said to the doctor, as he furrowed his brow in perplexity.

"Been there before? You mean déjà vu? That's honestly fairly common, Joe. It may seem strange, sure. But, it's nothing to get worked up about. Why, just the other night, I had a dream I ran into this old beggar lady who used to live in our area. At least I assumed that's what she was. She always wore this creepy black cloak. Like some kind of a robe. I was going to the parking garage right here, and she picked my pockets and stole my car keys. I was so mad I...well anyway, you get the point. I felt so silly once I awoke, and realized it was just a strange dream, and nothing more. Pure fiction. Not real" Dr. Boltzmann said.

"Yes, I understand. But still, the sensation I felt during the dream wasn't just normal déjà vu. I've felt that before, and am aware of that phenomenon, already. Who isn't? It's just that, when I approach the treehouse, I get this feeling like I'm returning to something. Almost like I'm returning home. But, it all just feels very wrong. I'm sorry, I'm not making any sense, am I?" Joe remarks, irritated by his own lack of coherency.

The doctor let out an amused chuckle. "Sorry, I don't mean to laugh. It's just that the fact you're now thinking about your dreams, is often a sign of returning to normality. I've seen it many times before with my other patients. Despite your concerns, I do honestly believe that you're making progress, and starting to get better" Dr. Boltzmann proclaims, as he breaths in, smirking.

"You've improved a great deal, even if you think you're not perfect. As to not making any sense, don't worry about that. It's fine. Part of my job, is attempting to make sense out of what people otherwise perceive as senseless."

"How about your medication? Do you need me to refill it? I can write you a new script right now, if you like" the doctor asks, beginning to reach for his pen. "No, not yet. I still have a few pills left. I've been cutting them in half anyway, so that should make it last a bit longer."

Concerned, the psychiatrist bit his lower lip, and shook his head. "But you'll be out soon, even so" Dr. Boltzmann remarked. "It's ok. I've only been taking it when I feel particularly sad. Usually a few drinks is sufficient alone to help me with that."

"You know that's not quite how the medication works. You're supposed to take it every single day. Ideally, at night. I would advise totally abstaining from alcohol in the meantime" The doctor instructs. "Is it dangerous, doctor?" Joe asks of his physician.

"If it's just a little, it'll probably just negate the effects. Excessive amounts of practically any medication is generally not a good idea, though" the doctor responds. Joe, didn't like his doctor telling him not to drink. He knew it was a bad idea to mix alcohol with medication, but he was an adult, and if he felt like having a drink every now and then, he damn well was going to do so.

"Truth is, I'm still not totally comfortable with these pills, doctor" Joe said, concerned. "Why's that? Have you experienced any more side effects?" Dr. Boltzmann asks. "It's not like before. When I decided to go off of them cold turkey. Not quite. But, yeah I have. Every now and then, I'll still feel it. That things don't feel right. Like I'm out of my body or something" Joe responds, uneasily.

"Yes. That's what we discussed before. It's a medical condition, but that doesn't mean it's permanent by any means. Quite the contrary, actually. I've had patients before who have felt the same sensation from other prescriptions, and have recovered from it. As frightening and uncomfortable as the side effects may feel, they're only temporary" the doctor said, trying to deliver his answer in a reassuring tone.

"The condition is called Depersonalization-derealization disorder. Depersonalization, is when the patient feels like they're not real. Derealization, is when they feel like the environment around them isn't real. Going off of some medications abruptly, can cause it. Your medication's an SSRI. It's a selective serotonin reuptake inhibitor, so it's something you would need to taper off if it's to be discontinued" the doctor calmly replied.

"I know that. At least now I do. My kids

though, I'm concerned that they're dealing with the same level of anxiety though. No offense, but after what I went through, I don't want to drug my kids up on any more meds they might not even need" Joe tells his doctor. "They're just kids, and if an adult like me had such a difficult time managing something like that..." Joe cleared his throat, and began talking in an increasingly contemplative tone. "Well, I don't want to even think about what it would be like for them. To cope with and have to endure the same hardships. Children, shouldn't have to worry about stuff like that. They're strong boys, but I want them to have as happy of a childhood as they can. Well, as happy as could be at this point. Considering all that has happened, that is" Joe concludes.

Dr. Boltzmann nods his head, in agreement, after hearing his patients words. "I understand. That's your call as a parent to decide. Even though I don't think the medication would harm them, it's still your call. I always try to respect decisions regarding my patients children" Dr. Boltzmann, responds.

"Speaking of my sons, that reminds me. I'm thinking of taking the kids to their grandma's house for a few days" Joe says, with his voice sounding more optimistic. "Good idea" the doctor responds, smiling. Joe, found the doctor's smile unsettling. It was well intended of course, but his toothy smile reminded him of the beast that took his son away from him.

"I think I should be heading out now, doctor. Could you give me your card again? I'm not sure I have your new number" Joe asks. "Of course," answered the psychiatrist. The doctor takes out his wallet and casually retrieves one of his business cards out of it.

Joe's eyes twitched nervously as he noticed the unusual leather his doctor's wallet was made out of. Not just normal leather like the couch he was sitting on. It looked like some kind of snake skin. Perhaps maybe even, alligator or crocodile skin. Joe took the business card, and quickly headed out to his car in the nearby parking garage.

"Boy, am I glad that's done with" Joe mutters under his breath, as he unlocks his car door and gets in the vehicle. Taking a breath of relief that his session was over and done with, he turns on his car radio. Joe's house wasn't too far away from the doctor's office. In fact, it was probably walking distance. He enjoyed driving though, and this seemed to take his mind off of things. Which was particularly needed, on this especially stress inducing day.

Joe had been listening to the radio while in his car, and the news broadcast was about halfway through, when he was suddenly taken off guard by what he heard on the radio. "It's been about one year since the tragic incident involving a young boy at the Illusion-Zone Resort..." Abruptly, Joe switches off the radio and curses under his breath. His heart pounds heavily, as his agitation spikes.

"Fucking assholes. Why do they keep talking about this? It's been a year..." His thoughts continued to race, beating himself up over the agonizing matter. Like a maggot in wood, or a moth in clothing, his contemplation gnawed at his mind.

"What was I thinking? Taking my kids on a trip on Halloween of all times? I'm about to do it again, now too..." Joe, thought as he quietly considered if he should just call off his family's trip to their grandma's house.

"No, that's silly. It's just any other day. A coincidence. There's nothing really supernatural about Halloween. It's just the 31st day of October. Nothing more. Nothing less..." the man tells himself, as he pulls into his driveway. Beginning to cool his temper, Joe enters his home.

The rest of the evening was largely uneventful, for Joe. He and his two boys Rafe, and Jimmy, were settling down in their comfortable home in the Midwest. Thinking of his two surviving children, Joe manages to calm down a bit more. The troubled father, tells himself in private, that he needs to stay level headed for his children's sakes. That his sons, must be unbelievably stressed. Although stress, merely began to describe it's maddening intensity.

Joe, had experienced the worst thing a parent

ever could- A child, taken away from him. Not merely just killed. Eaten alive. The deaths of loved ones upsets us all. More than that, the lingering effects of his son's death haunted the man, relentlessly.

He had heard of people describing the loss of a loved one as feeling like being on a roller-coaster. It's not though. A lot of people can't comprehend what it's actually like. It's not like being on a rollercoaster watching life unfold, It's like being the roller coaster and not knowing what a rollercoaster even is or what on Earth is going on.

After dinner, and quickly downing a few shots of whiskey, Joe retired for the evening. His kids were still downstairs. Jimmy, the younger boy was watching Teenage Mutant Ninja Turtles on the television, and his older brother, was trying to do his homework. Looking annoyed, Rafe, shouts at his little brother. "Could you turn that off!?" Startled and confused as to why his older brother was so irritated, Jimmy complies, and switches the television set off.

At the base of the home's staircase, Joe prepares to go off to bed. "God, I could use another shot" he mutters, cracking his neck. Despite just having had a few drinks, the man begins to contemplate having another shot. "No, I'm already overdoing it," the man thought as he remembered his behavior the night before.

22

It started off normally enough. He had been sitting at his local tavern with one of his buddies from work. Drinking, having some shots with his co-workers. Something that he used to do for fun, but now found himself doing as a necessity to prevent himself from completely loosing his marbles. To stop his mind from deteriorating into a state of sheer madness.

His co-worker and friend, had assured Joe that things were going to get better. The man had patted him on the back, and smiled. Joe knew he had meant well, and it was just a friendly gesture, of someone reaching out to him.

"I must've had one too many..." Joe reflects. In response to his friend, Joe had cut him off mid sentence when he was attempting to comfort him, and smashed his own beer glass down on the bar table. The glass shattered, and soaked his hand in blood from the broken pieces of glass.

"Thing's aren't the same anymore. Everything's wrong, and gone to pieces..." Several pieces of broken glass remained in his hand. Joe clenched his fist tightly, which cut the glass into his palm.

"What was I thinking? I behaved like an asshole last night." Joe now glances at his hand, which was now covered in bandages. Joe grabs a couple of pieces of candy corn, in a Halloween candy-jar near the nightstand and heads upstairs toward his bedroom.

Trying to sleep, Joe lied restless in bed as he similarly did these past 364 nights. "I guess this is at least better than the nightmares" Joe thought, as a sudden image flashed in his mind. It was a grisly image of a crocodile insatiably chewing on his dead son's bones. He reached over to the whiskey bottle next to his bed and grasped it in his hands looking at it, intensely.

He knew that drinking wasn't the answer, but at least it seemed to dull his torment. "I can still picture it. Like it's burned into the back of my eyelids" Joe thinks. The man remembered back when they found what little remains were left of his son. The eyeless skull. Eyes, plucked right out. He turns his attention once more to the bottle, and takes a large gulp from it. Joe closes his eyes and rests his head back down on his pillow.

Seemingly mocking him, the grandfather clock in his room strikes midnight. It was officially now October 31st. The day he dreaded most. Joe used to love Halloween as a kid growing up. It always seemed harmless. A carefree day children spent having fun. Now, as a grown man, he'll forevermore associate it with tragedy. With the day his youngest son, was viciously taken from him.

The hands of the grandfather clock continued to tick away. Even the incessant ticking of the clock reminded him of his son's death. Like that story in Peter Pan. How the villain in the story "Captain

Hook", would panic and freak out every time he heard the ticking of a clock, since a crocodile had eaten his hand with his watch on it.

Joe, had also realized the cruel irony that his dead son's name was Pete. Furthermore, the name of one of his two surviving son's was Jimmy. A coincidence, honestly. It didn't occur to him till after the incident. Jim, "Jimmy" which his son went by was short for James. Captain Hook's name was James Hook. He and his late wife had known of the vague connection. But now, the matter just felt too strange and overwhelming to him.

It had felt like life was playing a sick joke on him, and that his life and dead son, were the punchline. That his life, was nothing more than a mean-spirited joke told by some asshole in poor taste. The kind of joke school-kids would make up. "And the costume he wore..." Joe muttered in grief, thinking about the green tunic his son had worn for the costume.

The situation had reminded Joe of something he had learned in philosophy class, years ago in his youth. It was something about a logical paradox. About a crocodile, who captures a boy. The creature, tells the boy's father, that he will release his son, if he can guess what the crocodile will do. The boy's father, answers correctly. That the crocodile, will not give him back.

Irked by his own thoughts, Joe reaches over for

a jar of earplugs. He retrieves two out of the container, and puts them in. "Try to think happy thoughts..." Joe thought to himself. "Happy thoughts, like in the storybook. Happy thoughts, like Peter Pan would do when he wanted to fly away to Neverland." Within a few minutes he successfully manages to relax and dozes off to sleep.

Chapter 4: Premonition

October 31st. Halloween. The day at last has come. Joe's two young boys were just finishing up school. They were sitting in their principal's office, after being told by their homeroom teacher to report there after class at the end of the day.

"Are we in trouble?" inquires Jimmy. Rafe, smirks in an attempt to mask his true melancholic feelings, at the moment. "No, I don't think so..." the older brother responded. He had an idea he knew why they were called there. While still young, he was a bit older than his brother, and felt he managed to connected the dots. They went to a Catholic school, so they were probably going to talk to one of their priests or nuns now that it was the anniversary of their other brothers death. Their brother Pete, who was the youngest of the three.

"What's that? Something you're reading for class, Rafe?" Jimmy asks pointing to a book sticking out of Rafe's backpack. "Huh? Oh, yeah. It's something by an author named Dante" he explains picking up the novel.

Rafe opens the book to a bookmarked page. "It's called The Divine Comedy, I think this is where we left off in class" he says with his finger pointing to a page. "I've never heard of it. What's it about?" Jimmy asks. "Well, I'm not finished with it yet, but it's pretty good so far. It's an old book abou-" Rafe says, stopping midstance. The young man, quickly returns the book to his backpack and turns his attention to the front of the room. "Oh..." Jimmy exclaims, in a startled manner.

Their conversation, had been cut-short, by the sound of whoever it was that summoned the boys to the office. The room's door briskly swings open, and sure enough one of the school's priests enters the room. Alerted by the priest's presence, the two boys, quickly stand up. "No, please sit..." responds the priest, cheerily. The holy man closes the door, sits down, and gets right to the point. "Boys, I'm aware of the significance of todays date to the both of you" he says to the two brothers. "Yes, Father O'Reilley. I know, too..." grimaced Rafe.

Taking his older brother off guard, Jimmy's eyes welled up and the boy began sobbing uncontrollably. They didn't normally talk about it. Not regularly at least. But, did Jimmy not realize what today's date was till now?

"Is he really that dense?" wondered Rafe. "Jimmy, must've noticed all the decorations. Not to mention all the costumes the other kids were wearing. Maybe, he somehow had just forgotten that the tragedy had coincided on a Halloween. No, that's not the sort of thing you just forget. Maybe he just didn't like thinking about it that much." Rafe didn't know. He understood that his brother was younger than him, but he normally wasn't this sensitive.

"What the hell," thought Rafe. "Why was Father O'Reilley reminding us about this? Opening old wounds. He's doing more harm than good." It was reasons like that, that he had been questioning his faith lately. This self rightcous, bastard had just caused his little brother to cry. "How could he say something so thoughtless around us. To think, he's supposed to be a man of God..." Rafe thought, while he clenched his hand tightly. He felt like ripping that Roman collar off of him, and shoving it up his ass.

"I'm sorry. I didn't intend to make you cry" Father O'Reilley said placing his hand on the boy's shoulder attempting to comfort the boy. He had only wanted to let them know that he's here for them. Although, he can't imagine what they're going through. He went on about how they'll one day be reunited with their brother.

"When will that be?" Asks Jimmy. "When? Once we're in heaven, of course" remarks the priest. "So, not till I'm dead? After I'm grown up and old? I don't want to wait that long..." the boy said softly.

"Maybe if the Second Coming happens, in your lifetime, then I suppose it would happen sooner." Interested, Jimmy looks at the priest and holds back his tears. Father O'Reilley, didn't want to give the child false hope. He wondered if referencing scripture, would placate the young man. Since to some, accepting their hardships due to providence, was sometimes, more palatable. At least, compared

29

to the alternative- Senseless suffering.

"How will I know when that is?" Jimmy asks. Struggling for the right words to say to the child, Father O'Reilley reflects on the question. "I'm afraid no one really knows, my boy. Not even the apostles and disciples of Christ really knew." The younger boy looked down, unsatisfied by the priest's words. In fact a lot of people thought it would happen shortly after Jesus resurrected. Did you know that, my son?"

The boy did not. Neither of the two brothers did. The priest, continued in his explanation. "That's actually part of why it took so long for the scriptures to be completed. They didn't see any need to hurry up and rush writing the whole Bible, because they just naturally had assumed that Jesus would be coming back yet again within their lifetimes."

"So that's why the Bible has so many inconsistencies in it?" Rafe, interjected. The priest was taken aback. He had not anticipated such a bitter reaction from a child, but knew he had better not scold him at a time like this. He knew he needed to try to be understanding, as best as he could.

"A man of the cloth, has to be a pillar of composure" the priest reminded himself. He was well aware what these two brothers had gone through. His job as a member of the church, wasn't all just about reiterating catechism to his flock. The boys already have the dogma recited to them enough in their classes. Members of the community, look up to clergy like him, so he tried to take no offense.

"I know it can be difficult to keep your faith. Especially in situations such as yours. But, you must try. Praying alone, can work miracles. You boys need to keep that in mind. I'm not going to lie to you boys and say I have all of life's answers figured out. I don't. I may be a priest, but I'm still just a man. It may sound too simple to be true, but prayer really is the best thing to participate in right now. Sometimes, the simplest solution is the best one."

"You mean like Occam's Razor?" was what Rafe wanted to say to him. The philosophical principle which is used by many. The idea that the belief in some kind of a supernatural power, took too many jumps in logic, and was therefore an exceedingly irrational conclusion to reach. "What a hypocrite" Rafe thought to himself, not able to look the man in the eye, as he turned his head in revulsion.

With his anger boiling like a kettle, Rafe thought about the notion and impracticality of prayer. "Pete's long dead. He's gone forever, and the reality is there's no way they'll ever see him again. What good could come of prayer now?" Rafe dismissively thought to himself, rejecting Father O'Reilley's words.

He wasn't going to wallow in despair, but he also wasn't going to embrace superstition, and resort to talking to himself. "Why did I have to go to this religious school to begin with?" the young man thought. "Why couldn't my brother and I just go to a normal public school without all of this absurd indoctrination?" The questions ran through the boy's turbulent mind.

"Just try not to lose your faith" the priest said. God, loves you. "The reason bad things happen, isn't because of him, but rather because of The Evil One." Jimmy turned his eyes back at the man. It seemed the priest had caught his attention, by his cryptic words.

"The Evil One"? Jimmy repeated, inquiring as to what the priest meant. Father O'Reilley nodded. "Yes, Satan" the priest tells them. "Wait. You mean that he's actually real? Like in actual life?" the younger brother asks. Father O'Reilley nodded his head, again. "Yes, I'm afraid so."

"Sometimes his influence is subtle. But there are stories, both in real life and in scripture of him appearing in the real world" the priest says, in a sincere tone. "How can you tell if he's coming after you?" the younger brother asked, in a worried tone.

Father O'Reilley, thought back to one of his sermons, and continued his explanation. "Well child, he's usually depicted as having the head of a goat. But not exclusively. Sometimes, he appears looking like a serpent, or a dragon. Reptile like" the priest stops once he realized what he's saying.

"What about a crocodile?" Jimmy exclaims. "I'm sure that's just a coincidence. I'm sorry, I didn't mean to make you think of it like that" the priest says, somberly. "Can he appear as a person?" Jimmy, asks the priest. "Sure, sometimes. It's usually subtle though. Like appearing as a harmless child."

"A child? Why?" the younger brother asks, curiously. "To catch us off guard, Jimmy. To appear innocent. His innocence is feigned though" said the priest. "Like a pure evil Peter Pan," Jimmy thought to himself, creeping himself out, since Pete had been his dead brothers name.

The priest looks at his gold wristwatch, as the hands ticked away. "Ok, I won't keep you boys here any longer. The two of you may go" Father O'Reilley said. "Finally..." thought Rafe. Jimmy's tears, had finally dried and the two brothers left the room. "I wonder if my words were helpful at all..." the priest thought to himself, now in solitude.

"First he makes Jimmy cry, and then he scares him by talking. That's gotta be the most counterproductive counseling session ever..." Rafe thought as the boys began their usual walk back home. Their walk, was only a couple of blocks, and it consisted of a leisurely stroll through the neighborhood park.

"Rafe..." Jimmy said softly. "Do you really think Father O'Reilley is right? About the Second Coming?" Rafe's eye's jolted open in surprise. "I didn't expect him to ask that. How am I supposed to answer him?" the older brother asked himself, uncomfortably.

"Do you think it's true? You know. About Jesus coming back?" Jimmy asks him, sounding intense. "I..I don't know..." Rafe replied. "Damn it. That priest got him all worked up," Rafe told himself, in silent observation. Jimmy, said nothing, while closing his hand tightly. Clenching it, as if holding something important to him.

The idea seemed pretty far-out to him. Everyone, suddenly looks up in the sky, and they all see Jesus flying up there? He just didn't know how much of that he believed anymore. He didn't want to upset his brother, so he refrained from expressing his disbelief. They returned home, and noticed that their father had arrived there as well, which was unusually early for him.

"What do you have there?" asked Rafe as he pointed to his younger brother's hand. "You look like you're holding something, Jimmy." The younger brother looks over to his clenched fist. "Oh, this?" Opening his hand, Jimmy opens his palm to reveal a set of brightly colored beads.

"It's the rosary Grandma gave me" the boy said. Rafe, sniffs his nose, catching a whiff of the scented prayer beads. "They smell nice" Rafe said. The beads, had an aroma of rose buds. "Yeah, it does" Jimmy said, agreeing with his brother.

The scent, reminded them of spring, which was welcoming, as it was the dead of autumn. "They're from Pete's funeral, remember? Jimmy stated as the boy put the rosary in his pants pocket. "Right..." Rafe replied uneasily, in recognition.

"Dad's back sooner than he normally is" Jimmy observed, as they approached their home. Their father, was tending to his garden at the front of the house, watering the plants. The man appeared to be fairly calm, as he leisurely whistled a tune. "That's good to see him doing something other than drinking for a change" Rafe thought to himself.

Joe his father, had been hitting the liquor pretty hard, ever since Pete had died. Dad had taken up gardening in the past year, and it comforted Rafe to see that he was doing that upon returning home, as opposed to drinking away his sorrows. "I guess everyone needs a hobby, and doing so must've helped take his mind off of Pete's death" he thought.

"Of all the flowers he could grow though, why was he planting sunflower seeds? Does he realize it's fall now? Won't the flowers just die in this type of weather? If they even manage to grow at all, that is. I guess that part was irrelevant. As long as he's happy, it doesn't really matter what kind of plants he was growing," Rafe thought to himself, as the two brothers neared their home.

"Dad, it's late October. I'm not sure if sunflowers can grow in the fall," his older son said. "Oh, is that right?" their father Joe said, amused yet embarrassed. Scratching his head, the man breathed in an exaggerated sigh, demonstrating annoyance.

"What sick irony" thought Rafe. "Growing those flowers to forget your dead son, and now the flowers are just going to die on you, too. No, I'm being dumb. That has nothing to do with Pete." Rafe, averted his eyes, trying not to look at his father's gardening. "Damn it. I know it's Halloween, but why does everything have to remind me of what happened to him?" the boy thought as he and Jimmy walked up to their father and his plants.

Joe stood up, and tried to brush some dirt off of his jeans. "Damn it, I'm going to have to change out of this, I guess" the man said, unable to clean off the muddied pants. Anyway, how would you boys like to go to your grandma's house today? The younger brother's eyes widened with excitement. "Yes! That sounds awesome, Dad!" the boy exclaimed, in glee. Jimmy, invariably beamed up with anticipation the instant their dad mentioned their grandmother's house. He did, at least. Rafe, couldn't help but feel melancholic, considering the day's anniversary.

Jimmy, grew even more excited when his father told them that they're going to be staying there overnight. The boys, had loved going there. "Grandma, was a nice lady and lived in a really cool old house. But why tonight?" Rafe, asked himself. "We usually go trick or treating right after school.

Well, except for last year." He thought of his dead brother, but quickly shook his head, vanishing the disturbing thought from his mind. "It doesn't matter. We're going to Grandma's house, and that's reason enough to be enthused" the older brother reflected, privately.

"It's been a while since we've been there," Rafe thought, as he began to chill out. It had been for what felt like forever since they had been there. Of course, it was in reality only ephemeral in comparison to the length of time it had felt like. As does the duration of most occasions for children around their age. The three of them go inside their home, as the two brothers scurried up the stairs of the living room to their bedrooms and began to pack their overnight bags. It was only going to be for the day, but nonetheless, it felt like an exciting adventure to them.

A loud knock thumped, and catches the trio's attention. "Oh? Sounds like someone's at the door. I'll get it", said Joe. Their father, grabbed the door handle and nonchalantly opened the front door of their house. He was not prepared for the sight in front of him.

Someone with the head of a crocodile stood at their doorstep. "Trick or Treat!" remarked the crocodile. Of course, it wasn't actually a crocodile, or even an alligator. It was just some kid wearing their Halloween costume.

"Here, you go..." Joe says, as he reaches for the jar of candy near the door. "Thanks. Happy Halloween" replied the masked figure. "Happy Halloween, to you, too" responds Joe, unsettled. Closing the door, the man walked over to their kitchen and fixed himself a drink to settle his nerves. "Just one for the road..." Joe, tells himself, as he gulps down the liquor.

Dusk, sets in just as the children had finally completed their packing. They throw their backpacks into the back seat of the car, and hop in themselves. Their father, had only just turned on the ignition of the car, when a sudden feeling of uneasiness crept down their spines. Something felt off for some mysterious reason. All three of them had felt it, as if some sort of premonition. This sense of disquietude was fleeting, and they turned back to their usually carefree selves once their father had turned the radio on, distracting them from the worries of the world.

Discontented with hearing the "oldies" music station their father had selected, the children asked their father to find something else. Attempting to appease their request, their dad flips through several stations and comes across an old radio drama. They had tuned in toward the end of the program, but still decided to listen to it for the duration of the ride.

"How about this one?" Jimmy asks as he pushes the select button on the car-radio. Jimmy, had grown fond of listening to radio mystery dramas as opposed to music like most people. "What a strange kid..." Rafe, thought, looking toward his little brother.

"Thanks for listening to the words of our sponsors!" Booms the narrator, through the car's speakers. "We'll now continue with the stunning conclusion of our thrilling Halloween tale!" There was still some static in the audio, but it was still clear enough to make out what the program was saying.

The boys looked at one another, surprised. "Conclusion? Great, what luck" Rafe thought to himself sarcastically. He wasn't trying to be pessimistic. He was just annoyed that they're only now tuning in to the story. "How were we supposed to follow it by starting at the end?" the boy thought. He, like the vast majority of people preferred his stories the old fashioned way. In chronological order. If they didn't follow things sequentially, it was easy to get mixed up.

"The Phantom of Halloween", was the title. It was a bizarre mystery story which seemed to involve Sherlock Holmes. Ceasing their chatter, the three of them listened. "This shouldn't be a problem for the great Sherlock Holmes. This, should be child's-play. You are Sherlock Holmes, aren't you? asked The Phantom." Joe's curiosity had piqued. "The Phantom of the Opera, is in this"? their father asks looking puzzled.

"Childs-play, is exactly what this is, remarks Holmes, as he grabs The Phantom and tears the fiend's mask off", said the narrator. The radio drama continued with the narration blaring out the speakers. The radio host continues, "Silence fills the room. The Phantom, glances over at a mirror and gazes into it. He screamed, once he saw what was in the reflection. Still looking into the mirror, The Phantom basks in his own mirrored image. Not only was his face not deformed whatsoever, it was not even the face of an adult man, but rather the face of a young boy. He looks over at Sherlock. Holmes, seems to be around the same age, and is wearing an over-sized trench-coat, and an old fashioned hat, while holding a magnifying glass" said the narrator on the radio.

"Just then!" exclaimed the announcer, so loudly that it made Joe worry the blasting volume could blow out the circuits of his speakers. He wondered if he should pull over, but changed his mind once the volume returned to a normal level. "A woman's voice echoes out from the distance. Alright kids, come inside now and change out of your costumes! No more playing make believe. The children rush toward her! Who's trick or treating costume do you think was the best?, inquired one of the boys. They're both great. Now change out of your costumes, Halloween is over, and it's time to have dinner, then get ready for bed. The woman stated." Realizing the story had concluded, Joe turned off the program.

"What a strange Deus-Ex Machina ending", their father, stated. It's true they didn't know the context of the story, since they had just caught it at the end. However, the boys were familiar enough with the characters to know who they were supposed to be based off of. They were The Phantom of the Opera and Sherlock Holmes. Both classic literary characters. They supposed it made sense for that sort of program to be on during All Hallows' Eve. The bizarre plot twist, reminded Joe of the trick or treater he saw earlier in the crocodile costume. "Must've just been a coincidence", he thought to himself. "There's no way someone would do that to me on purpose."

"Deus-Ex Machina?" Jimmy, inquires with a bewildered expression on his face. Momentarily taking his attention off the car's wheel, Joe glances over at his son, and realizes Jimmy's unfamiliar with the word. "Oh, it's a Latin term. It means God from the machine. Like when a story has an unsolvable problem, and something unexpected like as if God himself steps in for it's resolution, to fix things" "Like when you pray to him?" the boys asks. "Yes, Jimmy", Joe, tells his son. "It was a plot device used a lot in old plays, from my understanding. An unexpected ending to surprise the audience" Joe

41

continued. "Oh, I see", responded Jimmy.

"Stories use the plot device, usually do so to pull off a resolution to a mystery. Sometimes it's obvious, or out of left-field. Unexpected. But other times, they hint at it early on. Sometimes, the best mysteries are ones that the reader didn't even realize were part of the plot. As if there were no real mystery to the story they had heard all along, and it was all part of a greater one, they didn't even consider. But, one that's hinted at." Jimmy turns to his father and opens his mouth as an epiphany hits him. "You mean like with foreshadowing, Dad?"

Impressed that his son was familiar with such a term, the man turns his head again, as a half-smile forms at the corner of his cheek. "Yes, Jimmy, foreshadowing. Sounds like you have been paying attention in your classes." Jimmy grins, proud that his father had taken note of his display of erudition.

"Yes, Dad. I-" Jimmy stops in the middle of his sentence and quickly points to the road ahead of them "Dad, look out!" the boy shouts, as Joe swerves the car to the side. The man, having been distracted by his son's remark had narrowly avoided striking a pedestrian. "Shit, that was close" Joe curses, as he steadily regains his position on the road, once more.

"Are you boys alright?" The brothers both nod their heads. "Yes, Dad" They reply, in unison like choir singers matching their tunes in perfect synchronization. "Who the hell was that?" Rafe, asks, turning his neck to view the road behind them. "Who knows" Joe remarks coldly, caring more for the safety and well being of his sons, and of himself.

"It was some old woman. At least, I think she was old. Hard to tell, because she was wearing some kind of a dark cloak around her. It looked like she was homeless. Probably crazy" the younger boy remarks. "Now Jimmy, you know that's not a very nice thing to say" Joe said, in a stern tone.

Just as he had finished his sentence, the man's own hypocrisy dawned upon him. He was unconcerned for that woman's safety over their own, so it struck him as ironic. Wanting to change the subject back to a more cheery topic, Joe thinks back to the radio program they had just heard. "So do you know about The Phantom of the Opera? Have you read that book in class or anything before? How about Sherlock Holmes?" the man asks his sons, as he forces a smile, feigning an more upbeat attitude.

"I know a little bit about Sherlock Holmes. He's a detective, right? I'm not too sure about the other one. I've only just heard of The Phantom of the Opera before. I know there have been movies about the character, but I don't really know much about him. Who was he? Was he based on a real person, like Dracula?" the youngest brother asks curiously.

Joe, contemplates for a few seconds, remembering how his own father had once read the story to him as a child. His dad- their grandfather, had quite enjoyed the story. "It must've been because he shared a name with one of the characters from it", he thought, reminiscing of a happier period in his life.

After reflecting, he then gives Jimmy a brief synopsis. "Real? No. He's fictitious. Sherlock Holmes, too. Do you know what that word means, Jimmy?" Joe asked the child.

"Of course, Dad. I'm young, not stupid. It means that person doesn't really exist" Jimmy, responds. "Right. Well, as for the book, it's been a long time since I've read it. But, from what I remember, the character's from an old scary story, where he terrorizes an opera house, and ends up dropping a chandelier on the audience" he explains to the boy.

"That sounds cool", responds Jimmy. Thinking about that story, Joe thought how it's conclusion felt like his own life right now. Just as that chandelier came crashing down on the people in that opera house, he had felt like all the misery of the world had gone crashing down on his own psyche.

Joe tried to stay strong for his boys, but truthfully he was at his breaking point. A man can only take so much. A hopeful thought pops into his head. "This trip will provide some respite for my nearly broken family." A smile forms on his face, and he looks over at his son as Jimmy returns the warm smile. Concluding their drive, Joe pulls their car into the driveway of their grandmother's house just as the bright orange sun began to set.

"Wow, the sun looks like a Jack O'Lantern right now", Jimmy, observed. Looking up at the sky, at the bright setting light, Joe nodded. "Yeah, you're right. It sure does. Almost feels like it's watching us from up there." Two massive stained glass windows peered down upon them from the top bedroom of the behemoth of a house.

Behemoth. The origin of that word, is biblical. From the Book of Job. Most people would assume "Genesis" was the oldest book in the Old Testament. However, they would be mistaken, as The Book of Job was written first.

Scripture tells of a "Behemoth" which watched over the figure Job during his tribulations. The mystery as to the identity of the figure, is disputed. It is described as a reptilian like creature in it's original Hebrew. Some, believe this to represent an alligator or a crocodile, while others believe it to actually be Satan merely masquerading as a scaled creature. "Job. Just one letter off from being my name" Joe reflected, silently. He had felt like his own life, was not dissimilar to that of Job's. His life also seemed to be plighted by misfortune and biblical lyricism as of late.

Towering before them, Joe, Rafe and Jimmy collectively admire the festive appearance of their grandmother's house. It's exterior, along with the front lawn appeared to be immaculately covered with elaborate Halloween decorations. A large Jack O'Lantern, and several other pumpkins, stood near the doorstep. While fake gravestones pinned into the grass and a fake skeleton sat on a chair on her porch.

All three of them, were very impressed that she still had found the time to do all of the decorating. Figuring that it must've been because she was old and retired. "With nothing better to do, she has all the time in the world to decorate at her own leisure" Joe thought to himself, as he and his sons, stepped up to the front door.

"Alright, boys. It's time to go in" Joe said, looking over to his two boys. Rafe, stood in silence, while Jimmy, smiled. "Yeah, ready or not, here we come, Grandma" the young man merrily said, as the trio prepared to enter.

Chapter 5: Arrival

The family prepares to enter the house, when Joe, notices an anomaly. "Odd. The door is unlocked" the man observed. Thinking little of it, as this was a fairly safe neighborhood, the three of them proceeded to go inside. Upon entering the house, the family was greeted by an unusual sense of humidity in the air.

"This shouldn't be" Joe thought, as it was October 31st in the Midwest and indoors. Their dad inspects a thermostat near the entrance, and looks at the numbers displayed on the device. After checking the registered readings, the man becomes increasingly perplexed once he observes that the device seems to be working just fine.

As if reacting to the trio's arrival, the temperature begins to shift. Within moments, the room's thick air, had shifted back to a regular level. The occurrence, oddly coincided with their entrance to the magnificent household. "Strange. But I guess it's nothing to panic over", the man thought, to himself.

The children unload their belongings from the car and go into the house. Knowing the place well, the boys attempt to get settled in, speedily. "Where's Grandma?" That was the question on all three of their minds. She clearly wasn't in the living room with them. "She was old, so maybe she hadn't heard them come in. Her hearing isn't what it used to be, and considering that Grandpa had passed a few years ago, he wasn't there to answer the door for her, any longer" Rafe thought, as he and his brother looked around the home's entrance.

Rafe missed his grandfather. He was old, so it wasn't as shocking to him when he passed, as opposed to Pete. However, he did wish he wasn't named after his grandfather. "Raoul", was his grandfather's name. Which was the French variation of the name "Raphael. Whereas, the young man just went by "Rafe." Of course, there were worse names to have, but this meant having to endure repetitive Teenage Mutant Ninja Turtle jokes from his classmates, forever.

The real origin of his name was biblical. "Raphael", was one of the angels who helped Michael the Archangel defeat Satan in the Bible. Kind of like the "Robin" to Michael's "Batman", in a sense. Of course, none of that mattered to most of the kids his age. They just thought of his name as one of the Ninja Turtles. An annoyance, which vexed the boy to no end. Thinking of the Ninja Turtles, only reminded Rafe of the crocodile that killed his brother, even though he was well aware that those are totally different creatures.

"What are you doing? You don't want to spoil your appetite..." Rafe scolds his little brother, as Jimmy shovels a handful of candy corn into his mouth. "It's Halloween, Rafe. I just want some of my candy before dinner" Jimmy responds, talking with his mouth full of the treats. "You're going to just make yourself sick, again", Rafe, says shaking his head in disapproval. "It's not like eating candy is the only thing we can do in the meantime. Just look at this place. Grandma's house is pretty big after-all."

"Yeah, it's huge. Okay, how about a game? Wanna play hide and seek?" asked his younger brother Jimmy. "Sure", Rafe, responded. The older boy paused thinking of the game. "Hide and seek. Pete used to love playing that game with us" he silently lamented. It wasn't just a game Pete liked. Back when he was alive, Pete had excelled at it. Immensely so. It was almost like Pete had a sixth sense when playing it. He was able to find his brother, father and himself so easily. "Dad hasn't played that game with us in a long time though. Maybe it was because it reminded him too much of Pete", Rafe, thought.

The two brothers, began the game. "Alright, let's play rock paper scissors, like usual to decide who gets to be It" Rafe says as he readies his hands. Counting down to three, the brothers play their moves. "Looks like I'm the lucky one" Rafe, teases. Having chosen paper, the older brother got to go first.

Although his brother Pete, used to be great at

hide and seek, he usually lost rock paper scissors. Pete usually tended to pick scissors for some reason. Rafe wasn't sure if Pete or Jimmy had ever managed to catch on that he had noticed. Closing his eyes, Rafe began counting to one hundred while their father finished up unpacking and proceeded to head into the kitchen.

"I'm going to go find your grandmother, and get dinner ready. You kids behave in the meantime" Joe shouts, carrying a bag filled with clothes. "Seems a bit excessive. Dad always overpacks" Rafe thought, observing his father's overstuffed backpack.

Rafe, covered his eyes and continued counting as his dad left the room in an attempt to locate their absent grandmother. His younger brother Jimmy, hurriedly ran out of the room, seeking to find a good spot to hide. Standing in the corner of the front-room, Rafe stopped his counting momentarily, and looked at an old painting near him. Looking at the painting, the boy remembers how the hanging artwork had always creeped him out. It had back when he was just a toddler, and it still did to this day. Just looking at it, made Rafe's hair stand up, as if the mystifying painting had radiated a paranormal aura.

It was an old painting, of a snake. At least, that's what Rafe's remembered being told, when he first asked about it when he was little. It was a snake, or at least some sort of serpent eating its own tail.

"Ouroboros" he thought. That's what it was called. The picture was supposed to be a symbol representing infinity. He never thought much about the painting before, but now that he was older the young man had found it to be especially unsettling.

A grisly visage of his dead brother's corpse, flashes through his eyes. Shaking the thought off, the boy looked away from the painting, sharply. "That reminds me of the crocodile, too. Damn, why did Grandma even have this thing in her house to begin with?" the boy wondered as he went back to covering his hands over his eyes. Nearing the end of his countdown, Rafe resumed the game of hide and seek.

"Ninety-Eight. Ninety Nine. One-Hundred. Ready or not, here I come!", shouted Rafe. "I don't think Jimmy's still hiding in the living room, or even in the kitchen. That would be too obvious, since that room is too close by. That wouldn't be a wise move, but then again he's just a little kid, so it's not impossible for him to make such a stupid mistake", Rafe observed to himself. After surveying the proximity of his starting location, the young man departs from the household's grand foyer, and makes his way to the other rooms.

The minutes crawl by, and after nearly an hours worth of exhaustively inspecting every inch of the house, Rafe was preparing to call it quits. This game had crossed over the fine line between exciting and boring. It was beginning to feel like a chore now. Annoyed, Rafe made his way to the one area he had forgotten to inspect- the guest bedroom.

Once Rafe turned on the lights, the boy's eyes quickly darted over at the corner of the room at an alarming site. "Grandma?" the boy called out. She was across the room, sitting in the top cabinet of one of the drawers. Rafe received no response from her. She didn't even turn her head to acknowledge his presence.

Instead, the old woman lowered herself further down into the shelf. As if in a trance, she began contorting her body like that of a ragdoll's. She twisted her torso till she was able to lower herself as far into the shelf as possible. Akin to someone jamming clothes into an overstuffed shelf. With only her hand reaching out of the drawer, the elderly woman stretched her arm outward, and inexplicably closed the shelf of the drawer with herself still inside.

The physics defying scene, had happened slowly, but ended with a loud clanging sound, as the shelf slammed shut. Rafe's ears rang, with a dull pain from the noise. The sound was so uncomfortable, the boy felt like bugs had flown into both of his eardrums, at the same time. It was like the same sort of uneasy sensation that nails on the chalkboard causes.

It gave him chills, and a sudden sense of dread filled the boy down to his core. Adrenaline overcame him, and gave Rafe a primal "fight or flight" sensation. Disturbed, he ran out of the room, slamming the door behind him. The boy tries his best not to lose his nerve, despite the frightful turn of events.

Rafe didn't know what to make of such a creepy sight, but something felt wrong. Thick moisture filled the air, and he noticed that the temperature felt eerily humid like it was when they first went into the house. Rafe, was back where he started in the living room, when something caught his eye. "Jimmy?" Rafe, said out loud, seeing a silhouette of who he could only presume to be his brother crouching behind a pull-out cot. "Dad must've setup that bed for one of us" Rafe thought as he approached the cot.

"Alright, I found you!" Rafe exclaims, relieved that the children's game was finally coming to an end. Just as his grandma did before, Jimmy's figure slowly began to creep his body downward, and then went under the bed. "Didn't you hear me? I said-" Rafe squats down, in an attempt to see his brother beneath the cot. Releasing a gasp in shock, Rafe finds that the bed had nobody under it.

With the intensity of a lightning bolt striking a tree, Rafe screams. He had screamed in both terror and confusion. Furthermore defying his expectations, his father, brother and grandmother all quickly entered the room. "What's wrong?" inquired his dad. "N-Nothing", Rafe uneasily responded, when he notices the situation no longer seemed amiss.

"Where have you been?" Rafe asked his brother. "He got tired of waiting for you to find him, so he started helping us prepare for dinner" Joe, responds for the boy. "How long have you been with them?" Rafe asked, as if interrogating the boy. Puzzled by Rafe's inquiry, his family looked at one another in confusion. "I dunno. Almost an hour, I guess" Jimmy responds. Rafe scratched his head, and let out a grunt in his increasing aggravation.

Together, the four of them proceeded to the dining room. While their grandmother's house had a myriad of spacious rooms, the dining room was rather quaint in comparison. The family, prepare their plates, and acquired the desired condiments. They were all ready to feast. Unable to wait, Rafe and Jimmy, pay no attention to their side salads nor soup and eagerly stick their forks straight into their chicken entrées.

Sitting at the head of the table, Joe crosses himself, and begins to say grace. Embarrassed, the two boys, drop their food back onto their plates, and join their father. Joe begins, paraphrasing a prayer with conviction. Abruptly, the man's words come to a halt, mid- sentence. "I wish I remembered how the prayer went exactly" Joe, says admittedly.

Jimmy, pulls out the rosary his grandmother had given him. The woman, looks over and notices Jimmy grasping the beads. She smiles. With her eyes closed, and her hands folded together, she decides to chime in. Looking contemplative, she finishes the rest of the prayer, verbatim.

Joe, Rafe and Jimmy, were all immensely impressed that she had recited it all just from memory. They quietly marvel how despite her age, she still seemed to have her marbles about her. The brothers, both went to a religious school, but even they struggled to remember the verses of the prayers they're taught in their classes. "Father O'Reilley, would be proud", remarks Joe, as he glances at his sons. The boys both nod, in agreement with their father. Afterward, they all gave a toast and enjoyed their supper.

"Did you pick up that medicine I mentioned to you?", the grandmother asks her son. "Yes, I already put it in your bathroom. I hope it works" the man, answers her. Smiling she says, "Thanks. As you know I'm old and tend to go to bed around after I eat." Joe, stood up and began clearing the dinner table. "That's fine, Mom. Let me know if you need anything. Even if I'm asleep. Don't hesitate to awake me if you need to, for whatever reason" Joe tells her. The elderly woman, stood up and set off to bed before the rest of them.

"Seems like Grandma is going to bed earlier

and earlier", Jimmy remarks once the woman had left the room. "That's just part of life, Jimmy. We all do as we age" Joe tells his son. "But Dad, you and Rafe still stay up pretty late, sometimes" his son remarks. "Not by choice, Jimmy. That's typically just something you do when you're younger, because you have the luxury of it" his father, explains.

"Even so, you boys should probably try to do the same. Even if you're not tired, it's still a good idea, just so you can get in the habit of doing so" Joe says, looking at his watch. "Why, Dad?" the boy continues to inquire. "Because Jimmy, the two of you had a long day. Doesn't Halloween normally make you feel wiped out? It sure makes me tired" Joe tells him, as he lets out a yawn.

"Not to me", Rafe thought. "Not till Pete died. Dad, just wants us all to go to bed, and get through this day, so he doesn't have to be reminded of it, any further. I can't blame him though. I want to get this day over and done with, too" the young man thought to himself. Having cleared their plates, the three of them heed their father's word's, and head off to their bed's. "Are you going to sleep on that pull out cot, Dad?" Jimmy asks. "Yeah, I think I'll be alright with that" Joe tells him. "Alright. See you later, Dad" Jimmy says, waving as Rafe silently strolls off to his own room.

Chapter 6: Metamorphosis

"Grandma Evita", is what they sometimes called her. But she usually just went by "Eve", most of her life. Preparing for bed, she went about her usual routine of taking a shower and taking her medications. One of which happened to be a skin cream she had recently gotten a prescription for.

The woman, had developed shingles. It's fairly common for elderly people to develop it. Having never received the vaccination before, she didn't think it was anything to fret about. Eve, thought to herself "How strange. The shingles, it doesn't feel like a normal sore, or infection. It feels sort of like I'm touching a fish. It kind of reminds me of fish scales. Or the scales of a reptile, perhaps."

"Ah, it hurts" the woman remarks, taking a bandaged pad off her waist. Now exposed, the sore was a much deeper shade of red. It has started out as a burgundy shaded discoloration. As the condition had progressed, it was now nearly black. Eve, was worried it had grown infected. Inspecting her rash, she gazed in repulsed awe. The afflicted area's scaly appearance, had become increasingly pronounced. Uncomfortable and exhausted, she took her usual sleeping pills and plopped down on her bed. Tossing and turning within minutes, the elderly woman's movements were like that of a rattlesnake.

Like a child's rattle, the old woman's shaking

reaches it's apex. A deep haze, fills her room as Evita springs out of her bed. Her whole body was now covered in the scale-like sores which she thought was a mere case of the shingles. The festering blisters, bubbled out of her pores head to toe. Horrifically, Eve's eyes bulge nearly popping out of her sockets. Her strained eyes, now looking more like those of some kind of reptile than eyes of a woman.

Shrieking, as if she never shrieked before, she screams. Feeling too big for her own mouth, her tongue, flops out of her throat. The poor woman's tongue, had swelled up triple the size of a normal human tongue. Long and shaking, her tongue oozes with slimy sludge, as the droplets of her saliva dripped onto the floor.

Piercing the October night sky, the woman screamed, yet again. Dread and despair, engulf her as never before. Eve's cries of terror, eventually wither away. Her moaning fades, to nothing more than a faint hissing sound. Her cold nearly lifeless body lies on the carpet, coiled up like a snake, with her tongue sprawled out, dripping a dark and murky fluid.

A cacophony of her agonizing screams had scarred the purity of the once tranquil evening. An unspeakable metamorphosis was transpiring deep within her. Although, they were the cries of a woman- the individual formerly known as Evita, if one were to lay eyes on her now, the term "woman" would no longer be accurate. She no longer bared any resemblance to her old form. The aforementioned lady's body had twisted to a deformed monstrosity. As if hypnotized, she, prepared to embrace her sinister fate.

Standing back up, with little strength, she slips and tumbles down from her bed, helpless. Attempting to lift herself up with one of her mangled appendages, she looses her grip, and slips once more toward her dresser. A shadowy presence, looms over toward her, smiling with dark glee. Eve, remained on the floor, nearly senseless. The shadowy apparition's smile, swells up with malice.

The air in the room turns ice cold. Drooling, Eve gazes at the ghastly figure with dead eyes. The perpetrator, exits the room. Closing the door, the woman was left to bask in the darkness. It was Halloween night, and the trick was on her.

Moving forward, the shadowy presence moves toward the grand foyer. Joe, Rafe and Jimmy all remain in their bedrooms. With the three of them sleeping, they remained blissfully oblivious to the terror which had just unfolded. "Time for hide and seek" the ghoulish phantom remarks, as the entire house is overcome with darkness.

The creature, creeps to the nearest room. Jimmy's room. Slithering like a serpent, it creeps through the crack below the boy's door. A shadowy cloud materializes and hover's over the sleeping boy's bed. "He must be thinking happy thoughts", it whispers. Placing it's shadowy hand over the boys head, the being enters Jimmy's dreams, turning his peaceful slumber into a nightmare.

Chapter 7: Nightmare

"I'm gonna find you!" Jimmy shouted, out loud. Looking over his shoulders, then dropping to his knees, his eyes peer back and forth. "No one there, either" the slumbering child thought. Unaware that he was asleep at his grandmother's house, he playfully explored his dreamscapes. After looking under the bed and couches, the boy approached the staircase, being projected by his unconscious mind.

"Are you upstairs?" the child cries out, trying to locate his brother. "No, I'm not!" gargles a distorted voice. Bewildered, a look of recognition comes across Jimmy's face. Startled, the boy's eyes twitch. He considered briefly calling back. After thinking about it, the boy reconsidered responding to the unfamiliar voice. "That's not Rafe" Jimmy told himself. Thinking quickly, the boy rushed to the nearby bathroom in seek of cover.

Looking at the storage closet in the room, Jimmy contemplates his position. Seeing no alternative, the child hastily swings the door open and jumps inside. "That voice that called out to me. It wasn't coming from human vocal cords, that's for sure. Wait, what am I saying? Of course it was. What else would it be coming from?" the boy fears, as his thoughts are silenced by the creaking floorboards. "He's coming up the stairs" Jimmy thinks, wondering if he should get out of the cabinet while he had the chance. "No. There's simply no time." the boy thought as he cusses under his breath. Jimmy, tries to concentrate on the noise downstairs. The boy focuses, and attempts to discern what it was doing. The slow shifting noise changed its pace. "Sounds faster. It sounds like it's pulling apart a shelf. Or maybe a closet. Is it looking for me?" Jimmy, thought in silence, and dread.

A shrill cry of anger booms from down the staircase, invading Jimmy's eardrums. The boy, trembles. "It's angry" Jimmy thinks, even more afraid. He hears a loud thud, as if the figure had thrown something in frustration. "Sounds like it threw something big. Maybe the refrigerator. Or a bed. What could that have been?" Within seconds, the same sound is heard again, as if the item were picked back up with ease and thrown once more.

"That's not possible..." Jimmy thought to himself. "It's strong. Too strong, from the sound of it. It would normally take at least a few full grown men to lift and throw something to make that much of a ruckus. What could be making all this commotion?" he contemplated, as it's strength, seemed inordinately powerful.

"I'm being silly. Of course it has to be human", Jimmy tells himself. Just as the boy was finally starting to convince himself that nothing out of the ordinary was truly going on, the voice from before calls out again. "I hear you!" shouts the voice with demonic vigor. The hair on the boys arms and neck stand up in fear. "Something is very wrong. That voice sounded like static. Like it was coming from a television with poor reception. Or a radio with a bad signal".

"Could it just be that Grandma or Dad had left the TV on? Maybe that's all. No. That wouldn't explain the thuds vibrating from the floor. Unless she had new speakers for her TV" the boy continued his thoughts as he tried to rationalize the situation.

"I'm coming, Jimmy" the voice blurted out once more, as if telepathically answering him. Just as Jimmy had thought he was making sense out of the noises, the voice solidifies his former worries. That had settled it. "There's something very bad downstairs" the frightened boy thought, now feeling like a cornered helpless animal.

The experience, had made him think back to when he was a little kid. A memory he had near some sort of treehouse. He didn't remember where it was exactly, but he remembered playing with ants and other bugs near the grass. Pulling off their wings, and limbs. It had seemed so cruel now in retrospect, but to a little kid it had felt like harmless fun.

His current situation, didn't feel that dissimilar. However, Jimmy felt he was now on the receiving end of the torment. It had felt like the scary voice from downstairs now, was tormenting him just the same. If there really were a monster downstairs, was it simply having fun with him? Or did it have ill intent? Jimmy, did not know and the uncertainty haunted him.

Closing the closet-door as tightly as he could, the boy listened. The footsteps began pacing again. Only this time, they had now begun going up the stairs. One after another, the footsteps crept. The movement was at such a slow rate, that Jimmy wondered if it was deliberate. It reminded him of the cautious inching of a caterpillar as it grew closer to him.

A slight crack remained at the edge of the door. It's not fully closed, but maybe he won't be noticed. Jimmy however, can still see a bit from out of it. Just slightly. The footsteps reach the top of the floor. They then come to a halt, as an eerie silence fills the room.

"Where did it go?" the boy contemplates, wondering if the coast is clear. "No, he's still there. It's not like it could have just vanished" he thought to himself. Right when he's about to check for himself, the stalking menace emerges.

"It seems like it's trying to mask its footsteps", the boy thinks as he witnesses his stalker walk by. "Where are you?" the predatory figure whispers, as if knowing its prey is close. "I know you're here. You can't hide. Not from me, Jimmy" it taunts as it tenderly strolls by his line of sight.

Looking through the crack in the door, Jimmy catches a glimpse of a tall dark figure walking by. The pace it was walking at, was more akin to floating at this point. Movement so brisk, it wasn't making even the slightest noise. If Jimmy hadn't already heard it call out to him from the floor below and made all that ruckus, Jimmy wouldn't have even detected it. "It's almost like it gave me a heads up that it was coming. Like it wanted to give me a sporting chance" the boy observed. The thought scared him. If that were true, then he was merely being toyed with.

"Too dark to tell who it is. It's big. Not a kid, and no adult I know. It can't be Dad or Rafe, that's for sure" Jimmy thought to himself, as he silenced his thoughts. "It can't hear me thinking, can it?" the boy wondered. "Maybe it can?" he wasn't sure.

The figure let out a howl. Too beastly sounding for a man, yet not animalistic enough for a beast. The sound was caught right in between the uncanny valley. Just off enough to seem unsettling.

"The uncanny valley." It was a term Jimmy had only become familiar with recently. He remembered hearing the word in art class. He and the other students, were all putting together a class project. The term, meant something appearing to be unnatural. Something which might resemble some human characteristics, yet are not quite convincingly realistic. A sense, that gave a feeling of unreality.

Quaking in fear, Jimmy lets out a gasp. Realizing what he had done, the boy quickly covers his mouth with both of his hands. Quick, but not quite quick enough. The figure shakes as if startled. Had he heard him? Terrified, Jimmy took out his rosary, and began praying.

The dark figure, leant in closely toward the closet. "Has it found me?" the boy wondered. It was right where Jimmy was hiding. Now mere feet away, it stalks ever closer till it's next to the door Jimmy was hiding behind. If it were not for the door separating the two, they would be nearly face to face. "I wonder if it can hear my heart beating?" Jimmy thought, as his heart pounded in his chest. The frantic beating, reminded him of the ticking of a clock.

Dumbfounded, Jimmy continues looking back at the figure, as it begins backtracking it's steps. It had leant back up, and returned to the base of the staircase. "It's walking away?" Jimmy, was confused, but thankful. The footsteps of the lurking figure, begin to fade away, as the boy continued to wonder where it was heading off to.

Chapter 8: Hide and Seek

"My hand!" exclaimed a terrified voice. Joe, glances downward in terror as he see's a cauterized stump where his left hand used to be. Growls and child-like giggles fill the darkness. With no direction, the man begins to run.

"Is it even still Halloween? What had happened to my mothers house? "Am I dead?" These are a few of the thoughts which had been going through Joe's tormented mind. He didn't know how or why this was happening. Maybe, there wasn't a reason. Regardless, their simple trip had turned into warped nightmare.

"This is disgusting. There's mud everywhere" Joe mutters as he examines his bare feet. "What is this junk? Where is this? Where am I?" his racing thoughts continue, as he inspects his surroundings.

Footsteps, echo down the darkness of the abyss, splashing through the filthy corridors. "Come out, come out wherever you are" shouts a sinister yet youthful voice. It grows closer and closer as if it were a missile homing in on it's target. "W-What. No. It can't be" thinks Joe as the giggling grows louder, nearly looming over him.

The voice, sounded like that of a monster. "A monster" Joe said to himself. He knew it sounded ridiculous, but it was the only way to describe it. Something was wrong with the tone he had heard calling out to him. Something was off. Yes, it sounded like a child, but it was too dark. Evil. He had never thought a tone of voice, could actually sound evil, before. Not till he heard that voice.

Anxiety overwhelms Joe like never before. A panic attack. "More than a panic attack", thought Joe. A mental breakdown. The man had always wondered what one had felt like. He thought he had one when his son Pete had died the year earlier, but he managed to pull himself together through that.

The urgency of the situation brought a tear to his eye. He was having a mental breakdown, and this is what having one felt like. "Never in my life have I felt so helpless. I feel like a character in a horror movie. One of the expendable characters, about to get killed off by some horrible maniacal monster. Normally, I'd dismiss such thoughts. But, not tonight. That voice...it sounded like pure hatred. This really was a monster, and he's coming after me" the man thinks wondering how he can possibly persevere.

"Whatever it is, it's so close, it practically feels like it's breathing down my neck behind me at this point." "I found you!", thunders a voice chilling him to the bone. Such playful yet dark laughter. "Whoever this is, he seems to be enjoying it as if he were a child playing some sort of game."

It wasn't as simple as that though. Although Joe's hunter did indeed seem to be having fun, there was a tint of malice in his voice. Maniacal. Like the voices you'd hear imitated from people working in a haunted house. The people dressed as monsters. Except, this was much more alarming, because it's usually adults you hear making those voices. This voice, definitely sounded significantly younger. It's youthful tone, made the calls much more unsettling.

"He's right across the hall from me now. It's too dark to tell who it is, but I can make out that much. How did he find me so fast? He must have this place memorized or something" Joe thought, as a disturbing epiphany rang in his mind. "Even if he did have this place memorized, how the hell could he have known where exactly I was? This person- this monster was like an omniscient predator toying with it's prey. Like a naughty young child cruelly burning helpless ants with a magnifying glass on a hot summer day."

"A summer day." How Joe wished that were the case right now. It sure as hell wasn't summer. Not even daytime. It was the dark of the night on Halloween, and Joe was neck deep in unadulterated terror. The stalking figure, continues splashing through the muddy water. "Damn it. It's right on top of me" Joe thought, realizing that he's cornered. "A dead end", thought the man, as he hopelessly turns around, not yet ready to face death.

Splashing forward, Joe hears the footsteps now casually walking toward him. Shining through the darkness, Joe sees piercing eyes looking back at him. "It just can't be..." he tells himself, privately. As if a blazing torch in a cave, the glowing eyes illuminate the corridors as it draws evermore closely.

"You're not very good at this game are you?" Joe's stalker mocks. "We can play something other than hide and seek, now that I've found you. "How about rock paper scissors?" the monster menacingly taunts. Glistening a radiant glow, Joe manages to make out what the figure was holding. "Scissors" Joe observes. The gleaming light, reflecting off of it's blades, takes Joe's mind off the dark dungeon. His tranquility proves to be fleeting, as the monster strikes him in the shoulder.

Stabbing deep in his flesh, the man squirms. "I can feel it scraping against the bone..." Joe thinks to himself. "As creepy as this kid is, he's still just a child, isn't he? This is life or death, and I have to protect myself. Is it a demon? No, just a figment of my imagination. It has to be."

"I might be handicapped with the loss of one of my hands, but I should be able to overpower him." Shaking in both fear and pain, he grabs the menace by it's shirt collar and prepares to throw whoever it was off. "So fast" Joe thinks to himself, regarding his attackers speed. He gets in a couple more stabs with the scissors, most of them barely penetrating Joe's skin. "It is a child. A boy. This can't be...." It was still too dark to tell, but Joe feared he knew who it was.

"Oh, you're so strong" the mysterious menace taunts, amused. He clenches Joe's remaining hand, and tosses the man aside like a child, throwing an action figure across the room. "This is impossible", Joe thinks to himself. "It's just a kid" he laments. Joe, feels a sharp pain in his abdomen, and coughs up blood.

Although the boy's aim was fairly reckless, he managed to strike a pretty nasty blow to Joe's stomach. His attention turns to his hand, as Joe notices he happened to rip off a chunk of cloth from his assailant's outfit. It was green fabric. "No...I was right" he weakly thought to himself. Feeling like a bug about to be stomped by a boot, the wicked child stood over him.

"I can't believe it. It's my son. No, not Rafe or Jimmy. It's the dead one. It was Pete. It's him..." Joe thought to himself. "My God", the man exclaims, shocked to see the boy's mutilated face. "The same face I saw a year ago, when the remains of his body were found. His eyes were gone. As if the crocodile had shucked them from his sockets, like oysters. Only two pitch black holes of darkness remained, where my sons beautiful green eyes used to be. As green as the crocodile who took his life."

Joe, thought to himself that his eyes must be in the same place as his soul. In heaven. "This place though, is not heaven. Not paradise. Is this supposed to be my own personal Hell? The eternal torture chamber prepared for me, for failing to protect my son?"

Dark laughter, explodes from it's mouth, yet again. "His teeth...these are not the teeth of my son. Pointy fang like teeth. Like a crocodiles... and his outfit...he was wearing a green tunic. Like Peter Pan, in the storybooks. The same outfit he had gone trick or treating with, on the day of the incident. He had thought it would be funny because of his name. He never took himself too seriously. Always wanting to play games, and joke around. He even wore it to the resort, afterward." The tunic was still ripped and stained in his blood. Just like before. Just like on that fateful All Hallow's Eve.

"He looks like my son, but the voice creeping out of his voice box was not his. Not Pete's. It sounds similar, but it was still off. That part was different. This can't really be him."

"Think happy thoughts...", the boy hissed.   His tiny hands squeeze at Joe's throat with supernatural strength. Looking at the small arms grasping his neck, Joe notices that the boy still has large crocodile sized bite marks on them. Just as Joe think's his adam's apple is about to be crushed, "Pete" slowly forces the man's face down into the dark murky water they had been scuffling in.

Joe, hears the boy clicking his tongue

repeatedly like a clock as he lowers him down. "I'm drowning" Joe, tells himself as the sludge begins to fill his lungs. Joe, makes a futile attempt to gasp for air, as the filthy rancid water flows into his mouth. With what little strength Joe had remaining, the senselessness of it all, raced through his mind. Now fully submerged, bubbles float upward toward the surface of the murky water, as Joe prepares to meet his maker.

Blackness fills the man's vision. Joe, had blacked out, momentarily. When Joe had came to, he was relieved to have been freed from his undead son's clutches. "W-What?" Joe, says coughing up a mixture of mud and blood. "Where did he go?" Joe mutters as he attempts to stand back up. He was injured and light-headed, but somehow still alive. "That's not really him. I refuse to believe that's actually my son. It must be a demon. My son would never do this to me."

Once his world stops spinning, Joe finally manages to catch his breath. The man, sits back up, and is greeted by yet another grim visage. Pete, or at least the thing that looked like Pete, remained lifeless in front of him. The pair of scissors Joe had been stabbed with, remained deeply thrusted into his the boy's side. "It had all happened so fast, but he must've been impaled by it in our struggle" Joe observes.

The father's heart sinks, as he felt an all too

familiar feeling. It was the same sensation he had felt a year ago, when he found out one of his son's had been killed. A tremendous sense a loss. The feeling of losing one's child. A feeling no father or mother should ever have to feel.

Once more, the man is overcome with grief. "No. It's not really him", Joe tells himself as he walks away from the tragic sight. He didn't know where he was heading, but he was eager to end the nightmare once and for all.

Chapter 9: Terror

"What's this?" Jimmy lifts his bare foot, and brushes moist orange sludge off of his heel. "Looks like the inside of a pumpkin", the boy observes. Leaning against the wall, he continues to brush the rest of the remaining mush off of his feet. "It's pointless", he remarks, when he notices that the fluid encompass the entirety of the ground around him. "Huh?" His attention turns to the wall he was leaning against, as slime oozes from out of it.

The foul gunk, wasn't just the on ground, but all over the walls, too. "Yuck" Jimmy says as droplets of the orange goo drip onto his forehead. "It's everywhere" the boy mutters, noticing it on the ceiling, as well. Stringy orange strands of mush hang from above him. "It's like the guts used to make pumpkin pie" Jimmy observes. The boy grows increasingly nervous. "Where am I?" he calls out, in desperation.

As difficult as it was for him to believe, he had no choice but to evaluate the strange situation he found himself to be in. The entire place, wherever he was, appeared to be like that of a pumpkin. The kind he had carved himself a week before with his brother and father. It was as if he were in the inside of a Jack-O'Lantern.

A faint thumping noise catches the boy's attention. Left with no sense of direction, the confused child follows the point of the noise's origin. Uneasy yet curious, he marched steadily through the mushy fluid as the thumping grew increasingly louder. "It sounds like the beating of a drum", the boy thought.

"Wait, no it sounds more like a heart beat..." The thumping, increased in volume and began beating more rapidly. Beating now, almost as if mimicking his own hearts palpitations. "A dead end" Jimmy mutters. The boy appeared to be lost, when he noticed an enormous cluster of the orange strands he saw before.

In front of him, stood a wall of the stringy orange cords. Similar to those one would find when taking off the stem of a Jack-O'Lantern. The boy, pulls them apart and forces his way through to the next room. Looking around, Jimmy notices that it was nearly identical to the room he was just in. The exception being, there were now several larger of the strands. Those of which, now resembled large towering pillars, littered throughout the area. "It's like a cave", the boy thought.

With what little light remained in the room, Jimmy leaned in closely to examine the pillar like structures. The boy held back a scream from the pit of his stomach. The pillars, looked almost like bones. Not just any bones. Ribs. Curved to the sides in a deformed fashion, they were unmistakable in their formation. It was as if they had been ripped out of a giant's chest, and the orange mush, was the leftover, uncleaned gore. The thumping noises were now so tremendous, that they were shaking the vicinity of the entire room. The corridors, trembled with the vibrations as the boy contemplated his next move.

Shimmering like a gem, a grotesque sight constricts Jimmy's formerly dilated pupils like tiny pieces of candy corn. The boy gasps. He could not believe the sight before his quivering youthful eyes. It was a heart. A beating heart. One that was freakishly oversized. Almost as if it were self aware and had noticed the boy's presence, the heart had begun to start beating irregularly. The change in it's rhythm, seemed as if it were panicked. Beating much more rapidly and loudly, like a bomb about to go off in a cartoon.

The heart's color, was likewise a deep orange and connected to the strands above. The fluid dripped from it, as if it were it's life- blood. Like a strike of lighting, the heart beats it's last palpitation. It erupts with the orange muck, and gooey chunks of it splatter on the child. Jimmy screams, and runs out of the room without even thinking about what dreadful terrors await him in the unexplored depths of his nightmare.

Chapter 10: Despair

"Dad!" The boy's frightened demeanor and loss of composure perished as he became elated to see a familiar sight. It was his father, Joe. "Dad? What's wrong?" There of course, existed a great deal of things wrong at the moment. However, Joe knew what the boy was referring to. Jimmy, wanted to know why his father was lying down on his side. Not only that, the boy wanted to know why his father was crying.

"Jimmy!?" Shouted a confused and overwhelmed Joe. "W-Wait! Don't look!" Joe, turned around, about to attempt to cover both the yet dead again corpse of Pete, and to conceal the mutilated stump where his hand used to be. Shocked, Joe notices that both his pain and the dead body of Pete, have vanquished. "My hand. It's back?" The man, did not know why.
Relieved, Joe leans over to his son, and places his hands on Jimmy's shoulders. Things didn't make sense, but he was happy to see him. Happy, despite the nefarious circumstances.

At first, thinking it was the phenomenon known as a "Phantom Pain" the strange occurrence where an amputee inexplicitly feels the sensation of their lost limb, Joe glances at his formerly wounded wrist. His hand, had once again become reattached to his arm, with no indications of any prior harm. "Dad, what's going on?" asked Joe's extremely confused son. "I don't know, Jimmy" answered Joe, as he hugged the boy. The two cautiously walked onward through the flow of filthy pumpkin guts, eager to escape their odyssey of madness.

"An exit"? Both the father and son, rejoice as they see a door. It's appearance was jarring and out of place considering the bizarre labyrinth they've been navigating their way through. Although, if they were to make a list of all of the things that seemed out of place this night, it would've been low on their concerns. They put their reservations concerning it on the back-burner, and approach the door, wanting to put these uncomfortable memories away, forevermore.

"Where are we now?" chimes the boy. The two of them assess their surroundings. There appeared to be some sort of seating arrangements. "What are these for?" the father and son both thought to themselves. A faint metallic scraping sound is heard, and they turn around quickly. "Dad, I heard something." "Me too, Jimmy" they remark, not sure what to anticipate.

"Jesus" remarks Joe, as he shields Jimmy's eyes with his hands. It was difficult to see due to the lack of light. However in the darkness there stood a row of crane machines. The sort of game you'd expect to find at an arcade or an amusement park. The kind where you put a quarter in it's coin slot, and maneuver around a metal claw for grabbing and picking up prizes. Usually a toy, or doll of some sort.

What remained in the machine's display case did sort of resemble dolls, but they were something else. Something disturbing. A sight, which Joe did not want his son to see. He didn't even want to see it, himself.

The machines contained tiny dead babies, in their display case. Some of which, were still only fetuses. They were piled on top of one another in the horrific crane cabinets. Row after row of them. "Jimmy, let's just keep going..." Joe tells his son. "What? What is it?" Jimmy curiously asked. "Just trust me and keep going" his father responds, still covering his son's eyes as they walked past the horrific scenery.

"What could that be?" Joe gently whispers to his son, as they hear shifting noises at the end of the hallway. "More seats?" the man says tilting his head. "What are these meant for? It almost looks like some kind of train stop. Or a bus stop" Jimmy says, peering through his father fingers. Joe, removes his hand now that they're past the gory sight. A mysterious voice booms and the duo turn around facing it.

"Yes, indeed. A waiting place. Waiting for a ride that'll never come. A way out, they'll never have" says a towering figure. Jimmy holds back a scream, as Joe steps back in shock. "Where the hell did that thing come from? It's so big, but I didn't hear a thing."

"W-Who are you"? Joe asks uncertain as to if this figure is friend or foe. The figure crept closer, not making a sound despite it's gigantic lumbering size. What Joe and Jimmy saw made their hearts sink. It wasn't a man. This creature, was a walking talking pile of dead infants. All of which, were stitched together forming the shape of a man.

"You're familiar with Limbo, are you not?" inquired the beastly figure. "Limbo? Like the game you play? Where you try to walk under a stick?" Jimmy innocently asks.

The figure scoffs at the boy's naivety. "Not quite, child. No, Limbo as in the dwelling place of those met with an unfortunate end. Where the souls of the just, are fated to go. Most of them exceedingly young children." The knitted collection of dead babies twitch and wiggle as the giant lifts it's arms, pointing at the empty seats. "Please leave. Your time has not yet come" the ghastly figure states. "Oh, thank God" Joe mutters, to his son, as they near the end of the room.

The father and son wander on, as the line of empty seats vanish. "Dad, this place looks different" Jimmy remarks. The boy was right, the room which they've currently found themselves in, no longer looked like that dreary train stop.

What are those things, Dad?" asked the boy. Two more monsters appeared from out of the darkness. They looked nearly like men, except much larger and appeared to be rotting. The two monsters, pointed to Jimmy and his father and laughed. "What sort of Hell is this now?" Joe thinks to himself. "Ha, he thinks this is Hell", one of the demons says. "These things can read your mind?" Joe thinks, as it seemed that indeed was the case.

The demons laugh. It was an oddly amused sort of laughter. Not the mad cackling Joe had begun growing accustomed to in this nightmare. "You don't remember?" spouts one of the demons, slapping it's knee in amusement. Joe shook his head. "Remember what?" Their laughter continues. "I wouldn't have thought demons capable of being so well humored. Especially, not in Hell..." Joe thinks, forgetting his thoughts are no longer private.

"This is not Hell", states one of the demons, as it tries to hold back it's laughter. This place is a shadow of what waits in Hell. This is Purgatory. You're here of your own doing. Of your own volition." "Of my own doing? What do you mean by that?" Joe asks of the demons. "You made a covenant to remain here. Forever you'll stay here. Your chances of entering paradise, have been sealed shut. You'll never enter it. However, you'll also never leave this place" says one of the demons.

"That's crazy. I would never agree to that. I have no memory to agreeing to such absurd terms" Joe tells, the demons. "Oh, of course not. While the suffering here may be miniscule in comparison to what awaits in Hell, it's still too much for a mortal man to cope with" says one of the creatures, no longer laughing.

"Don't you see? Of course you've forgotten. It's the way your simple mind deals with the loss. The way it deals with the agony. Your mind, eventually breaks and forgets. How many times do you think we've had this conversation? I assure you, this isn't even the last time we'll have it. I don't just mean with you, but also of all the rest of the poor souls who reside here", the other demon said chiming in.

"They don't seem nervous at all, or anything like that. Not that these demons would have any reason to be nervous. But they don't seem like they're lying. Could it be true? No. Satan is said to be the Prince of Lies. There's no reason to suspect his minions would not do the same" Joe thinks, as the beasts smirk, having heard his thoughts.

"I don't believe you" Joe tells them. He says this to them out loud, knowing they're reading his thoughts, anyway. "Yes, we know. You've said so before" the creature says, as Joe and his son prepare to carry on their journey. Walking away, the demons begin to laugh, yet again.

"Where did they go?" the boy asks, as the

demons fade away into the darkness. They were gone, but their incessant laughter lingered a bit longer till after they had vanished. Joe looks around the labyrinth, still expecting to find a way to make some sense out of this horrible place.

The demonic chuckling eventually ceases, and the pair approach yet another door. An unpleasant thought emerges in Joe's mind. "What was the point? We have no map or any way of navigating" the man thinks, in frustration.

"This direction could lead anywhere for all we know. It could lead back to where we started." Pessimism, had begun rapidly stirring in the man's mind. He was beginning to lose hope. "I have a feeling this way is going to lead out, Dad" Jimmy says to his father.

"Yes, son. Me too" Joe tells the boy, as he feigns an optimistic grin. Even if he was starting to feel despair, he felt he should attempt to stay strong for the sake of his child. He had felt enough hopelessness for the two of them, anyway.

As the duo approaches a door, a foreboding ticking sound begins. "Dad, I think there's something in the water" Jimmy says, as they look down at the putrid liquid that they've been tirelessly treading through. The dirty water, bubbles, and growls sounding as if the pits of Hell itself were having indigestion. A splash flows upward, covering the two with the sludge. Like a demonic jack-in-a-box, a figure lunges from out of the foul abyss.

It was that monster pretending to be Pete, again. Still possessing the visage of Joe's dead son, but now appearing even less human like. Sharp claws, where his fingers should be, and a long lizard like tongue springing out of it's throat. It widens it's mouth, with it's sharp fangs staring back at both Joe and Jimmy.

The frightened father and son, gaze down into the blackness of it's throat. It was like an endless pit. Just as represented symbolically in the Ouroboros, the darkness seemed to last for all of eternity.

"Was it just playing possum, before?" Joe thinks, not knowing how the fiend had managed to rebound from before. Joe had thought he had killed it, but it had returned seeming revitalized.

Lunging forward, the monster, bites down on the man's hand. Joe lets out a cry of despair, as his son watches in horror. What Joe felt was worse than the agonizing pain he was in, was the fear he had felt just then. The fear, that he was about to see the death of another son.

Scared, Jimmy cries out for his father. Thinking quickly, the boy notices a pair of scissors lodged in the creatures side. Jimmy, seizes the opportunity, and pulls the scissors out of the creature. Before it can retaliate, Jimmy holds the scissors upward, and slices the scissors across the beasts chest.

Jimmy's strike was successful. The creature winces, and Joe was now freed from it's clutches. Joe, stumbles, dazed, yet his hand free. He had been released, but he was disoriented from the impact of the monster's attack. The man attempts to re-gain his composure, but his disorientation intensifies. "Dad!" Jimmy shouts, as his father falls to his feet, unconscious.

Looking closely, Jimmy can see that the blow he had struck was very large. A dark fluid spurted from out of the chest of the creature. The blood, looked much like how pumpkin pie did. Mushy and brown, with an almost orange tint. Laughing, the creature wags his finger back and forth in front of it's face, as if to indicate "Nice try."

Opening it's mouth again, the monster's tongue springs out and wraps around Jimmy's neck. It pulls him closer as the boy wrangles around helplessly. "He's about to eat me" thinks Jimmy, as he frantically reaches in his pocket.

An idea popped into Jimmy's head. It was a last ditch effort, but Jimmy searched through his pockets and pulled out the rosary his grandma had given him. "I wasn't sure if this would even still be in there. Glad something still makes sense, in this nightmare" he thinks as he grabbed the beads. In desperation, the boy took aim, and threw the beads down the creatures throat.

It had seemed like only something that would

work in movies, but the idea did indeed stop the creature. At least it had, momentarily. Dropping Jimmy, the fiend grasped it's own throat, and began coughing violently. It's pumpkin pie-esque blood, now gushing out of it's empty eye sockets, like streams of waterfalls.

Regaining consciousness, Joe's eyelids slowly opened. The man reaches over and he grabs his son's arm. "Let's go!" Joe shouts to the boy as the two of them take advantage of the creatures loss of composure. They knew it was time for them to prepare to escape.

"Okay, Dad", the boy replies, when Joe notices Jimmy covering his shirt. A red stain formed underneath the boys hands. "You're hurt?" says Joe, as his son collapses. Beginning to panic, Joe grunts as the mix of unpleasant emotions continue to rush through him.

Their foe, rises again. Screaming in anger, the beast snaps the rosary between it's clenched fangs. The creature's eyeless socket's widen with fury. It rushes toward the father, and sinks it's teeth deep within Joe's waist. Joe, screams and Jimmy whimpers sadly. "I'm dying", the boy says as he uncovers his stomach revealing what he and his father both fear to be a mortal wound. "It can't end like this" Joe says. Jimmy weakly squeals, as color begins to drain from his face.

Mocking their despair, the monster chuckles as

more of the pumpkin pie blood gushes out of it's fangs. With all of his remaining strength, Joe strikes the creature straight in the jaw. His punch, was stronger than any blow he's dealt before in his life. Surprised by his own strength, he knocks several of it's fangs out, and sends the monster down to the murky ground.

"Nothing seems to stop it" Joe remarks in desperation. Joe, cracks his knuckles, thinking he had broken at least a finger or two with his punch. The adrenaline flowing through the man, was more than enough to mask the pain he felt, despite his discomfort. Rebounding, the creature readies it's attack. No longer having a feigned tone of humanity, it lets out a vicious animal like roar. Joe, takes it off guard this time, and tackles the beast. Both of them roll around in the filthy muck again, as the monster begins to overpower him.

Joe, reaches over for the broken rosary beads in the water. "It has to still be there", he thinks to himself, aware that the beads had an effect on the creature. His fingers move through the mushy fluid as he tries to locate it before the monster get's it's stamina back. "I found it", he exclaims in his own mind. Although, it's broken in half, the man had found it among all the putrid gunk.

Blood trickles down Joe's mouth as he prepares his counter- attack. "You're not my son. Go back to Hell" Joe says, firmly. Realizing what Joe was attempting to do, Pete's evil doppelganger closes it's mouth shut tight. "It's no use" yells Joe in frustration.

Thinking quickly, Joe looks at the menace's gouged out eye sockets, and shoves the beads inside the left one. The monster cries out, covering it's left eye. Now with it's guard down and only covering one of it's eyes, Joe does the same to it's other eye socket. The pain brings the demon to it's knees, and Joe relentlessly pummels the sinister being with every last iota of fight he had left in him. Joe, beats it's face in, till nothing remained but a messy mound of fleshy pumpkin pie like mush.

"Did that finally kill it?" thinks Joe. The frantic father grabs his son, nudging him to see if there's still life within him. "Not too late" The man remarks as Jimmy coughs weakly. "He's alive, but barely" Joe, picks the child up, and places him over his shoulder. With his world spinning and life spiraling out of control, Joe opens the door at long last. The two of them enter through, creeping into the next room. Joe was reluctant, but soldiered on. He was well aware that only more pandemonium, was likely in store for them both.

"Dad, why won't you play hide any seek with us anymore?" asks his son. "What?" Taken aback, Joe turns to the boy. "Is it because it reminds you of Pete that you don't want to play it?" Jimmy asks. A grimace forms on the man's face. "No, son. It's not that I don't want to be reminded of Pete. I could never forget him. Joe's says as his swelling eyes hold back tears.

"That thing pretending to be Pete though...It's like it's making a mockery of Pete. Making a mockery of your brother. Of his life, and what he meant to us. That's what I don't like." He takes the boys hand. "Let's go. No matter how bad this seems, I promise you, we're going to get out of this place. I'm not going to lose another son." A smile forms on the boys face, and they continue their path.

Their confidence, is cut short once the duo hears a familiar sound. "No more..." Jimmy says, as they hear ticking again. "No. It's not him, again. Look" Joe points in the distance. "Clocks? It looks...it looks like we're in some sort of a tower now. Barred windows appeared at the sides of the corridors. Their jaws drop as they look out of the windows in confusion.

"Where is this?" Jimmy asks. Not knowing how it could be possible, the two of them peered out of the barred windows and saw it lead outdoors. There appeared to be some sort of wooded area with a treehouse visible in the distance. Looking at it, caused them to feel overcome with an uncomfortable sense of familiarity. "This place" Joe whispered, indicating a sense of recognition to his son.

"Huh? What is it, Dad?" Jimmy asked of his

father. Joe turned his face to him "Nothing, son. Let's just keep going" "That was strange" Jimmy had thought. "It seemed like Dad recognized that place" the boy wondered.

While still on his father's shoulder, Jimmy attempted to figure out the mystery of that wooded scenery. "Have we seen that place somewhere before?" the boy wondered. For some reason, it seemed familiar to Jimmy as well. Although, the boy could not quite put his finger on where he had seen it before.

Joe, looked around the tower like structure. "This looks like some sort of clock tower" Joe said, as the two spot a collection of clocks on the walls. "They're all set to different times" The man observes, as he realizes the futility of trying to figure out what time of day it was.

Corpses appear in the steady flow of murky water at their ankles. Some of them, not quite dead. Joe glances at them. "Their faces..." He was disturbed at what he saw. Not just because they were dead. Because of the frozen expressions on their deceased faces.

"Those are not the faces of people in agony. Those expressions, were the faces of those in ecstasy. Why?" Joe reflects back to the chilling words of the laughing demons. "It was like they wanted to be there. Did these people, make the covenant those demons spoke of? If this really is

Purgatory, were these people overcome with joy knowing they're here instead of Hell?"

"They're just trying to trick me" Joe tells himself as he tries to think of something other than the unsettling notion. He had begun to think if he was just lying to himself at this point. About if he and his son, were going to make it out of there. Did he really believe that? Or was he just saying that to prevent himself from wallowing in despair? "I've hit my nadir, regardless" Joe thinks. While true, he cannot shed the demon's words from his consciousness. He had felt haunted before from the death of his youngest son. Now though, even that seemed like a paltry sorrow if this indeed was Hell.

Ticking ever more quickly, the clocks continue, filling the room with anticipation. An uneasy sense of dread consumes them, as the duo awaits whatever these clocks are counting down to. Like a volcano long overdo for an eruption, the clocks explode with ringing. Joe and Jimmy, cover their ears in pain.

A foamy fluid, trickles from out of their eardrums. "What's this?" Joe says, expecting to find blood flowing from his ear. Instead, he discovered a mushy pumpkin pie like substance. The same murky fluid they saw bleeding out from that monster who had taken Pete's visage.

The clocks cease their onslaught of ticking and tolling, as a woman's scream takes their place. "Where did she come from?" Joe asks himself. A woman, sitting on a stretcher stood across the room from them. She was covered in a hospital gown, and was leaning over toward her toes.

The woman's stomach bulged with pressure and she let out a hysterical moan. Sounding like a wolf howling at the full moon, she screams as blood erupts from her every orifice. Joe closes Jimmy's eyes again, fearful of the sight before them. Having seen it three times before when his son's were born, the man knew what was taking place. She was giving birth.

With a burst of blood, the woman births a child. Soaked in it's mothers blood, the newborn wiggles around and gazes at Joe. The head of a goat, stood atop the shoulders of the infant. The child lets out a deep growl. It's voice, sounded much too mature for a baby. It's screaming sounded more akin to that of a full grown man.

The howling, turned to sinister laughter as the woman grabbed the child and looked at Joe and his son. A ghastly thought emerged in the depths of Joe's mind. "Was this the Anti-Christ?" he somehow thought it must be.

"Were these horrible sights meant to deter them? Meant to throw them off track?" Joe wondered if that could be the case, since the past couple of demonic manifestations, did not pursue them. The monster masquerading as Pete, was a different story. The man did not know the reason, and he wasn't certain he had the time to contemplate the matter any further.

Seemingly only leading to darkness, the father and son carried on their way. The mother and her demonic son's cries and laughter, fade in the distance as the darkness grew blacker. "I can't see a thing, Dad" Jimmy exclaims. "I know. Me too, son." Light fills the room, and they're greeted by a familiar sight.

"Is that who I think it is?" Joe whispers to his son. "Yes, I think so, Dad" the boy excitedly shouts. "Y-Your wound?" Joe shouts out, as he looks over at Jimmy. The man glares down at the boy.

"Oh, thank God" Joe says in relief. His son's wound had disappeared. Jimmy, clutches himself in confusion. "H-How?" the boy wondered how it could be so. It didn't matter. Things were finally getting better for them. The duo, approaches the figure they saw standing in the distance, hoping and praying it was indeed who they thought it would be.

Frustrated by the turn of events, the ghostly menace pulls out of Jimmy's dreams and lets out an annoyed grunt. It peered down at the boys face. Jimmy was smiling. His nightmare, had turned to a pleasant dream, after all. The demon sneered, and hastily rushed out of the room.

Irritated at its failure at besting the two, the fiend turns its attention to the room across from Jimmy's. It was Rafe's bedroom. Turning his sights to Jimmy's older brother, the evil spirit enters Rafe's room, and just as it had done so to Jimmy, it floats over to the slumbering boy's bed and intrudes his dreams. Having infiltrated the child's subconscious thoughts, it begins to stir up another nightmare.

Chapter 11: Deus Ex Machina

"I don't understand? Where did everyone go?" Rafe shouts. He was at his grandmother's house a moment ago, but now he was in what appeared to be some sort of child-like amusement center. Filled with a wide variety of colorful tubes to crawl through. Sort of like the ones found in Chuck E. Cheese, or other playground areas like that. Except, this place had not been maintained very well. Quite the contrary. It was rundown and dimly lit, despite the colorful décor.

He didn't know how or why, but he was in the midst of it's labyrinth, on his knees crawling through one of the many tubes. The environment, was filled a couple of inches of cold, dark murky water. Or at least, what he presumed to be water. To make matters worse, that strange humidity he had felt earlier at his grandmother's house, had returned. It was thick, and filled the formerly stale air.

Time crawls by, as he tries to navigate futilely through the disgusting corridors. A sudden strike of trepidation runs downs his spine, when it dawns on the boy that he doesn't appear to be making any progress. Time continues to run dry, till he sees something in the distance. A weak voice calls out to him.

"It's no mirage, there really is someone there" Rafe thinks as he grows closer. Approaching the figure, the boy realized who this person was. It was someone he indeed recognized well. The man before him, was none other than his grandfather. Raoul, the man who's name his own was based on. "What? But he's dead" Rafe thinks as he came face to face with a man he hadn't seen for a long time.

Raoul, his grandfather, was curled up in the fetal position. The elderly man, did not seem to be fully aware of his grandson's presence. Slowly, he pulls himself together, and gently whispers the situation to the boy. "This is Purgatory", he weakly remarks. "I have been here every since I died, trying to find my way out. My way to heaven. I fear I'm going the wrong way, and going to the other place" he explains to his grandson. Before Rafe had the opportunity to respond, the lights dim, and when they go back on, his grandfather was gone.

"This must just be some kind of a nightmare" Rafe thinks to himself, trying not to panic. "I've got to wake up soon." He soldiers onward, seeing no other alternative hoping it's only a matter of time till he awakes from this horrible slumber. Rafe, contemplates "I don't usually have nightmares. Was it something I ate? Perhaps a fever? I don't know."

The temperature in the air inexplicably drops drastically. Rafe hears a faint buzzing near him. Flies. There were flies buzzing around him. He attempts to shoo the insects away, when he notices a wet substance on his hand. It was the murky water the boy had been crawling through. Somehow, it's gotten darker.

Rafe, leans in close to sniff his hand. A foul putrid stench, flows up his nostrils, invading his remaining sanity. He gasps for air, and vomits a bit. "Smells like shit" the young man thinks as he examines the filthy fluid. It was a deep dark red. Almost black. "Is this blood?" he asks himself looking at his fingers.

There was something solid in the murky liquid. Feeling through it, Rafe grasps a handful of it, and inspects it. Although it was dark, he was able to make out the identity of the content, once he held it closer to his face. "Candy corn? What's this doing here?" the boy says out loud. None of it had made any sense to him.

The little light, which remained in the room, flickered again. There were markings on the walls. "Was this hear before?" he wondered. Rafe, was fairly confident it had not been. "Strange symbols. No, wait I recognize these" thought Rafe. "Pentagrams?"

A voice whispers to the boy from the darkness. "Turn left. That's the way out." Curious, he does as it suggests, hoping it does indeed lead to the right way. As he progresses, the whispering continues.

For a moment, Rafe thought he had heard the voices of children. Their voices, were mostly inaudible, but it sounded like the children he had heard earlier when walking home with his younger brother. The trick or treaters. Their voices eventually faded, as Rafe continued his path. Now, only the other singular deeper voice from before remained.

The whispering voice, gradually turns to a chuckling laugh. Within moments, the laughter stops. Taking it's place, Rafe hears familiar cries. It was the same chaotic yelling Rafe had heard the day his brother Pete was killed. The sound of the pandemonium, from that last year's Halloween. There were so many voices, all crying in shock, and despair.

"What kind of amusement park has live fucking crocodiles in it, anyway? It's like a child designed that place. An idea a stupid kid would come up with" Rafe angrily thinks to himself. Thankfully, the haunting screams begin to fade, as Rafe notices a change in the dim lighting of the facility.

Slowly, Rafe could tell that the light seemed to be getting brighter. An orange light. Like that of pumpkin carved on Halloween. Not extremely bright, but enough for him to think that he was perhaps making some progress, after all. "I can't believe it. An exit!" exclaims the boy, in his own mind. He crawls out of the messy tubes, and into the next room.

"I never wanted to be here, again..." Rafe, observed the area further. He indeed recognized it. It was just as he had suspected. The area he now found himself in, was the playground he was at that fateful day. It's part of the amusement park he and his family had gone to. The place, was part of the resort his other brother was killed at.

"What's going on?" the boy shouts. He was disturbed to be reminded of more bad memories. "If only I were Sherlock Holmes, like in that radio story", he thought to himself. "Then, I might be able to make sense out of all this."

"Abandon all hope, all ye who enter here", read a sign on the wall. It was placed where the "Welcome" sign had been when he was last at this place. "Dante", Rafe thought, thinking back to a book he had read at school. It was from "Dante's Divine Comedy." What the sign at the entrance to Hell was supposed to read.

Rafe, looked around further. There were air hockey tables, arcade cabinets, dinner tables. The usual sort of things you'd expect to find at one of these facilities. The temperature had gone back to normal again, so he guessed that could only be a good sign. Cautiously, he approached the auditorium like area. It's filled with several tables, seats, and a stage with animatronic characters standing at the center.

At the top of the stage, there appeared to be an enormous grand chandelier. It had a large, old looking statue on top of it. Rafe couldn't quite make out what the statue was. It looked like the kind of statue you'd see at a church. "Another part of this place that never made sense, to me. I know this was supposed to have been an old church. But, why keep all these angel statues? Was it just because they thought it looked cool?" Rafe thought to himself, about the irrational design.

Bright orange flowers were neatly placed at all of the seats of the dining tables. They sort of looked like the ones his father had been planting in their garden. Although these flowers were dry and withered. They were dying. It looked like they hadn't been watered or cared for in a long time. Despite their failing conditions, they were still vibrant in their colors.

Looking more closely at the figures on the stage, Rafe found what he saw, to be very unsettling. The animatronic figures, all appeared to have animal heads. Not just any animals heads. Reptiles. Or maybe amphibians. The young man was unfamiliar with the distinction. At least, for all of them. A frog, an iguana, and a toad. The boy was able to discern that much.

The lights brightened the room, and the figures switched on, with their eyes glowing. It had taken Rafe, aback and he felt his heart beginning to race, as sweat formed at the top of his head. He brushed a few of the beads of sweat back, as he tried to figure out who had turned the contraptions on. "Hello? Is someone there?" Rafe calls out, hurriedly looking around the room.

Laughter erupts from the voice boxes of the machines. Rafe, begins to step back, and trips over something. "Huh? A Jack- O'Lantern?" He was positive that it wasn't there before.

The boy grew nervous, and assessed his surroundings, once he stood back up. Jack-O'Lanterns, had mysteriously appeared all throughout the room. Several of them, were set resting in front of all the figures in a neatly placed row.

Rafe looks upward at the lights on the ceiling, as their bulbs dim once more. With no explanation, the figures on the stage vanished before his eyes. "Did I hallucinate that? Rafe wondered, as he began questioning his state of mind. "Am I going crazy?" the boy thought to himself, as anxiety flowed throughout his body.

The room is engulfed by laughter. Benighted in darkness. Too dark to see what was in front of him. Pitch black silence pierces the darkness. Subsequently, followed by the sharp precise ticking of a clock. A garish glow illuminates the room. The light which filled the room, was a color Rafe had never seen before. A color he didn't know existed. Looking at it, made him feel uneasy. Like he had a migraine. Or how he supposed his dad must feel like when he has a bad hangover from a night of drinking too much.

Just as Rafe's eyeballs felt like they were going to burst from the sensory overload, the light slowly shifts to that bright orange shade, he had seen before. The orange glow reminded him of the pumpkin tinted setting sun, from earlier in the night.

Not believing his eyes, Rafe looked at the front of the stage in shock. A crocodile sat in a chair in the middle of the room. It sat, not as a reptile, but as a man. As if it were trying to be human.

Mankind always tries to anthropomorphize things by their nature. However, in this case, the crocodile sat in the chair with its legs crossed, just as we do. Contorting it's body in an impossible posture. Mocking our physiology, and defying the boys preconceived notions of reality by doing so.

The Jack-O'Lanterns, begin to rumble. They shake with intensity, as blood begins to drip out of their carved out orifices. Rafe's stomach begins to ache, and he feels pressure throbbing in his throat. The young man, coughs and vomits up a handful of blood splattered candy corn.

"You're just going to make yourself sick, again" the terrifying figure says to the boy. Rafe thought back to earlier in the day. It was taunting him. The crocodile was mockingly imitating what he had said to his brother earlier in the night for eating candy. What he had said to him, after they had finished playing their game of "hide and seek".

After wiping the blood from his mouth, Rafe

turned his attention to the figure on the stage, again. The crocodile, contorted it's face, creating a twisted human like smile. The whites of its eyes, filled with contempt. Seeing this, and everything that's happened so far, Rafe realizes that this isn't just any crocodile. It wasn't just some normal animal, like the one who ate his brother. This was far worse.

Rafe, didn't need any further clarification as to this figure's identity. It's mere presence, had shattered any ambiguity. It was The Beast. The Dragon. Satan, himself. Rafe thought back to Father O'Reilley's warnings from his descriptions earlier.

The frightful figure stretched its front claws out, as if they were the hands of a man's. Stretching out, as if to signal to the boy that the fiend had found him. It was the sort of motioning he and his brothers would make, when playing hide and seek. A gesture which was meant to tauntingly indicate "I've got you now."

An unholy visage now stared directly at him. It was as if it were perceiving the essence of his very soul. As if it had seen straight through to Rafe's former unbelief. It laughed at him.

It's laugh, was not in a playful way or tone like children make, or even as adults do when they've heard a good joke. No, this laugh was hateful and malicious. It was a laugh, which had reeked of malevolence, like none he had ever heard before. A dull pain jolted in Rafe's ears, as blood trickled slowly from out of them. Hearing this laughter, felt like a jagged blade was being scraped around in his eardrums.

After enduring it's venomous cackling, a chilling revelation, dawns upon the boy. "I'm going to Hell." Maybe he was already there. He never even believed in God before, especially after what had happened to his brother last year. That made him more than question his faith, and God's existence.

The palpable physical manifestation of evil in front of him, made him doubt that God even existed. But Satan did. He can deny that reality no longer. "Seek and you shall find." A biblical verse, which Rafe just remembered, back in one of his classes at school. It was a verse about how if you search for God, he will show himself to you. He hadn't done that. Maybe, if you don't it's Satan who looks for you, instead.

Despite his youth, Rafe realizes that any hopes and dreams he held before are over. Like Peter Pan in the story book, he will never grow up. Things have gone too far, and his fate couldn't be any more obvious. This is the end. His soul screams. He's erred gravely. The thoughts of despair echoed in his consciousness. An ice cold chill ran down his spine. A chill which said, "Tick Tock...Tick Tock."

Before he knew it, scaled hands had wrapped themselves around his waist. They latched on around his very soul. The beast squeezes fiercely as it begins to drag him down to depths which he did not know even existed. The proverbial serpent in the garden, had now become literal. It had become reality, and it had caught him.

Crocodiles, spin and spiral around once they've gotten their prey in their jaws. Just like the legendary Ouroboros. It spun down into infinity. Everything he had done, everything he had known was gone. The only thing which remained, was the ticking of a clock.

At least, those were the thoughts which flooded through his terrified young mind. Is this the fear Jonah had felt when he was swallowed by the great fish? Shaking with fear, and knowing that his soul would be torn asunder, imminently, Rafe thought of the hopelessness of his predicament.

"This is going to take a miracle. Like some kind of crazy way out, like what Dad said happened in those old plays..." Rafe looked upward at a window atop the room. "W-What's that?" Rafe asks, observing what appeared to be the sun and the moon both glimmering from out of the window. "Is that writing?" The words Yes, No, Hello, and Goodbye appeared alongside the glow of both the sun and moon, as a shadowy object made it's way across them. It seemed like the hand of fate.

To say things felt precarious, would be an understatement. It was much more dire. He feared his fate was perdition. As if it were the voice of the universe answering, the boy hears thunder. The entirety of the establishment rumbles, and the grand chandelier above began to shake. With thunderous power, the chandelier comes crashing down like the fallen tower of Jericho. It then slammed down to the front of the stage, crushing his reptilian adversary.

Engulfed by a cloud of dust, Rafe starts coughing incessantly. Once he finally calms himself down, and catches his breath, the boy notices he could hear the sound of a clock tolling in the distance. "Midnight?" Halloween was over. At long last, a new day had begun. It had seemed a fitting end to the grim holiday, considering all the events which had transpired. Rafe didn't know why, but it was as if the lighting strike, had something to do with the time coinciding with it now being midnight.

He gazed over at the wreckage, expecting to see a grotesque sight. Expecting to see a mangled scaled body underneath the chandelier. He doesn't. At least, not exactly. Instead what he saw there beneath the chandelier sat a crushed Halloween mask of a crocodile, along with a bunch of bloody candy corn.

A light gleams in, from behind the boy. He turns around, and at long last notices a door. It was as if the door, had suddenly been unlocked. Eager to escape the nightmarish facility, Rafe, swiftly walked toward the door. Without giving a thought as to where it lead, the boy swung the door open, and stepped outside. Once outdoors, he was greeted by the illumination of the morning sun.

"Dad? Jimmy?" Rafe remarks."What are they doing here?" Rafe thought. He wasn't sure why they were standing outside. He wondered if perhaps they were waiting for him. Rafe, approaches his father and brother, and felt a sense of relief. They too, seemed happy to see him. "Had they gone through something similar?" Rafe wondered.

After greeting them, they all turned toward the origin of the mysterious bright light beaming down upon them. All together, they turned their heads and gazed upward at the sky. "Look there" Jimmy shouted. There was something up there in the sky.

Rafe, focuses his eyes and concentrated. He attempted to make out what or who it was. Although, he had a feeling he already knew it's idenity, before he even looked up. "His..hands..." Rafe thought as his eyes widened. His whole body was enveloped in warmth, and he thought to himself that it was the brightest light he had ever seen. "The light's so bright. It seems like it lasts forever" Jimmy remarked.

Having been thwarted once more, the monster which had been invading Rafe's dream, howled. It had not anticipated this joyous rendezvous, as the outcome. With greater anger than any man has ever known, the fiend standing above Rafe stared down at the dreaming boy.

Grumbling, the vile monstrosity approaches the

fireplace. Impatiently, it picks up and grabs the poker, at its hearthside. Grasping the iron between its shadowy clutches, it prepares to strike the sleeping boy. The morning sun rises, and like Peter Pan's shadow, the ghoulish menace, fades away. A crashing sound, booms from Rafe's bedroom, and the boy at long last, awakens.

Chapter 12: Reflection

"Good morning, Rafe" says a cheery voice. Rafe, opens his eyes and is greeted by the sight of his grandmother standing at the foot of his bed. "Breakfast will be ready pretty soon. I hope you slept well" she says to him. The boy, looks around, still wondering if what he had experienced the night before, was really just a dream or not.

"Halloween is over" Rafe remarks. "That's right. It's November 1st now" his grandmother replies. A puzzled look comes across the boy's face. "November 1st. You know. All Saints Day" she tells her grandson. Grandma Eve turns her attention to the foot of Rafe's bed. "So that's what that noise was? I guess it came loose. Good thing that didn't fall down while you were under it. Could you and your brother help tighten its screws before you go?" she asks. "Uh, yeah sure Grandma" Rafe answers.

It had seemed the chandelier in his room had fallen down. "Is that why I dreamt about it?" Rafe wondered. "Close call. Grandma's right. It's so close to the bed, I could have gotten hit by it" the boy told himself.

"How did you sleep, Rafe?" inquires his grandmother. "Um. Fine" Rafe responds. "That's good. I had the strangest dream last night. A nightmare, actually. I'll have to remember not to go to bed so quickly after I eat" his grandmother says, with a chuckle.

"Anyway, I'm going to check to see how your father's doing in the kitchen" she remarked. "What are we having?" A mischievous look formed on her face. "It's a surprise" she said smirking. Rafe sat still in his bed. He was thankful the horrid night was over, but he was uneasy about facing the new day. "That was weird" the boy thought to himself. Rafe didn't know what it was exactly, but things felt off to him, for some strange reason.

The uneasy feeling continued to linger over Rafe. He was still half asleep, since he only just awoke, yet the feeling nonetheless grew steadily stronger. "What...what is this?" Rafe thought. It was a feeling that he had lost something. Not just loss. But a feeling that he had given up or traded something. Something dear to him.

The sensation continued as Rafe grabbed his head. He wondered if it was a sort of headache coming along. It had felt as if whatever he had given up, he had traded for something, which was worthless. Less than worthless. Insulting. As if he were beginning to come to terms with a horrifying revelation.

Rafe thought back to when his brother Pete first died. His dad in particular was having a difficult time coping. It wasn't just the depression and anxiety, there was something else to it. "What was it called, again? De...something...depersonalization?

111

Or was it derealization? Something about being so stressed, you felt like the world around you was fake. A weird feeling of unreality. Rafe wondered if this was the sensation his father had described before, back when he was going through it.

"Am, I still dreaming?" asked Rafe in his own mind. The feeling was overwhelming. It felt like he had lost his whole family, friends, home, everything that the boy had held near and dear to him. That it was all gone, and he got a pile of dirt in return. Something worthless. The worst part of it all, was that it somehow felt as if it were all his fault. As if he had known all along and was just pretending not to acknowledge it.

Feeling like he'd go mad if it went on any longer, he stood up, and rushed over to his bedroom's bathroom to get a drink of water. Rafe, leaned over and drank directly from the sink's faucet. He cupped his hands, and filled it with water, splashing it on his face.

The odd sensation had gone away. "Seems that did the trick" the boy told himself. "Funny to think that such a normal everyday thing like splashing a bit of water on your face could negate a weird feeling like that. I guess it's the little things in life that put us at ease sometimes" he thought, reflecting on the matter.

"Alright. The worst is over. Just settle down. Think about those meditation exercises they taught you at school after the accident happened. It worked then, so there's no reason it won't work now. But what on earth was th-" His thoughts were interrupted. Rafe looked in the bathroom mirror in front of him and screamed once he saw what was in the reflection.

Chapter 13: Confusion

Grandma Eve and her son Joe were pacing about the kitchen, preparing what looks to be a festive meal. "Looks like breakfast is almost ready" she said. "Sure, if you can call it breakfast, anymore. It's just about noon, Mom" her son, replied back to the elderly woman.

"What do you mean, dear?" The sun had only risen not even an hour ago" the woman said, raising an eyebrow in confusion. "Huh?" Joe mutters, raising his wrist to look at his watch. "How peculiar. That doesn't feel quite...it feels like I've been up much longer" the man said. His mother chuckles, "Oh, don't worry about that. Time going by faster as we get older, is just part of life. Wouldn't it be nice to be a kid, with little conception of time, again? Anyway honey, just keep cleaning last night's dishes and I'll get everything else ready."

Joe had never been a morning person but wondered why the day was feeling like time was dragging on much longer than usual. "Was it just that I have so much on my plate, as of lately? Maybe, it's some unexpected side effects from my medication. I'll have to talk to Dr. Boltzmann about that next time I see him. These pills can cause weird symptoms sometimes" the man thought, taking a deep breath.

He considered the possibility, as he scrubbed

away, at the dirty dinner plates from the night before. They still had chunks of the leftovers on them. Soapy suds of water dripped down from his hands as he continued his cleaning.

"Damn it. I need to stop thinking so much. I'm worrying myself to death at this rate. So, I had a bad dream? Big deal. I just need to eat and have my usual morning cup of coffee. The day just doesn't quite feel right otherwise. Hard to believe I ever managed to function so long without any. My kids don't ever need it, and I sure as hell didn't used to need it either in my youth. What was the saying? Energy is wasted on the young?" Joe thinks to himself, as he attempts to put his troubled mind at ease.

Joe placed his head and leant it back contemplating the quote. "Who was that who said that? Some playwright, I think. Someone I studied in my old theatre classes. That's what this feels like in a way. Like some sort of crazy performance."
The man's thought's, were akin to a wild storm, stirring about the autumn leaves. "It felt especially like that when the media got involved. Just two days ago on the radio. I can't believe they were still talking about it. Like my life is just some sick story they can tell for fun. There were so many wonderful things about Pete. He was an imaginative boy, who loved his family. But people will only remember him as that kid who got eaten by a crocodile. Tragic

deaths make people seem so hollow. As if it were their deaths, which defined them."

"Retreading a story, and exploiting it, just for the sake of publicity. It's only because it happened on Halloween, that they wanted to bring it up, again. As if it were part of some creepy story for people to tell during the season. Sort of like that radio drama the boys and I heard in the car. It's nothing like that. Damn it, I hate this fucking holiday" thinks Joe, as he places the now cleaned dish down, and picks up a dirty pair of scissors.

Taking a washcloth to the edge of the blade, Joe begins scrubbing the scissors. "That news anchor from the other day though...it still pisses me off just thinking about that station's broadcast. Well, my sons and I aren't puppets on some stage meant to entertain people. We're real thinking and breathing people, with feelings just like anybody else. Damn it." Distracted by his thoughts, the scissors slip out of his hand, into the sink.

Frustrated, Joe swears under his breath. "It's not just coffee I need. What I need now is some food. I always get irritable without breakfast. It's the most important meal after all" he thinks as his empty stomach grumbles.

"A good meal sounds heavenly after that nightmare I had last night. Pretty much anything would." An image of Pete happily standing aside him flashed in Joe's mind. "Heaven. Where I'll see Pete, again." It was something he longed for. "Not something I expect to experience for at least a few more decades though" Joe thought to himself as he turned around to his mother.

"So, tell me Mom, what's on the menu, anyway?" Joe asked as he sniffed the air in the room, attempting to discern the contents of the oven. Nothing was wrong with his sense of smell, but the origins of the savory aroma in the room, remained a mystery to the man.

"Oh, you'll see soon. It's a surprise." The words had not even left her mouth, when Joe had an alarming thought. A strange image, of a hypothetical meal had arisen in his mind. "Ha. That's ridiculous. That would never happen."

"Why would I even think that?" Joe thought to himself. She could be cooking anything. Why did such an idea...why did an idea like that even pop into my head?" The man's thoughts continued to stir, as the meal proceeded to cook. "That's so strange. That thought I just had, was so vivid. I wouldn't normally even think of such a thing."

The troubling image he had just imagined felt like it was projected to part of his subconscious. As if something were attempting to communicate with him, telepathically. "I don't think I've ever experienced anything like that before" he muttered to himself.

"What was that? Experienced what before?"

Grandma Eve turned and asked him, raising an eyebrow in bewilderment. "Oh, it's nothing, Mom" Joe replied to her. He was so tired, he accidently said what he was thinking out loud. Something else, that felt irregular for him. Taking note not to mutter his thoughts out loud, he thought like something was playing games with his mind.

Glancing over at the oven, Joe began wondering what resided within it. "Whatever's in there, is definitely more than enough to feed us all" he thought to himself. Joe starred at the oven. "I can't seem to recall my mother ever cooking anything of this caliber before. Not even when Dad and Pete were alive." The silly thought from before rose up in his mind as he stared at the oven.

"Can you at least give me a hint at what it is? By the looks of things, this is going to be quite a smorgasbord, huh?" Joe inquires. "Hints, Joe? I know you're curious but, no I don't think so. I don't want to give away the surprise. Getting this meal ready, wasn't an easy thing to do. In fact, it was quite an endeavor." Joe shuddered and halted his cleaning and thought about what she had just said.

"There's no way that...Mom, what do you mean by that?" What Joe had dismissed as just a silly thought, was now causing him to become legitimately concerned. Grandma Eve, simply giggled, ignoring his question. "Just get ready dear. The dishes are clean enough. Now go over to the table and sit down" the woman commanded of her son, pointing over to the dining room.

Joe, put the dishes down. His hands were still covered in soap, but he didn't care. The man's mind was focused on the enigmatic meal. "She's deliberately dodging the question at this point" the man thought, as his soapy hands dripped onto the kitchen floor.

Feeling like a scared kid at the top a rollercoaster about to go down a steep drop, Joe bit his lower lip in anticipation as he eyeballed the oversized oven. "Mom, please tell me this isn't what I think it is" he said, as he grabbed his mother's shoulder. "Hey! You've gotten soap on me now! I had better go change out of this..." She says brushing the soap off her apron.

Grandma Eve, walks off to change, leaving Joe standing in the middle of the kitchen, with his hands still dripping foamy suds. The man looked at the oven and contemplated his actions carefully. "Should I open it?" Joe wondered.

"Good morning, Dad" chimes Jimmy, as he enters the room. "How is it he can always be so cheery in the morning?" Joe wondered. "He doesn't even need coffee. I wish I could have that kind of energy..." he thinks to himself, once again envying his youth. "Hey, what's cooking in there? It smells good" Jimmy remarks, as he walks closer to Joe and the oven. Joe holds up his hand to the boy as he approaches it.

"Wait, Jimmy!" The concerned father quickly shouted. The boy jumped in confusion. "Is...is something wrong, Dad? I was just curious is all. I can help out if you want me too" the boy said to his father.

"Shit, how should I handle this? I need to get him out of the room quickly. But I don't want to freak him out. My reaction alone to the oven probably weirded him out enough as it is" Joe thinks, trying to figure out how to approach the predicament.

Joe looks at his son, and forces a smile. "No, everything is okay. I need you to go back in your room for just a couple more minutes while I get our breakfast ready with Grandma, okay?" Hesitating momentarily, the child nods. "Okay, Dad..." the boy replied and reluctantly headed back to his bedroom.

The young boy was clearly still in the dark about what had just transpired. But he had cleared out of the room, giving Joe the chance he was looking for. "Alright. Jimmy's out of the room. If there's really...if the thing in the oven is really what I fear it could be...then he shouldn't see it. I can't imagine the kind of impact...the kind of impression that would leave on a boy his age" the man thinks, as he prepares to tackle the awkward dilemma.

"Could it really be?" Joe, continued thinking, his mind now racing. "Is...is she really cooking...a crocodile? Or maybe an alligator, since those are legal to cook? If it is a crocodile, did she buy the same one that killed and ate Pete?" Joe thought. "I know she's old but...if she's done this, then she's really lost her marbles. Does she think eating it would serve as some kind of closure to us?" Joe wondered, now fearing his mother's mental state.

With his nerves this rattled, Joe hardly even needed his morning cup of coffee at this point, anymore. The man was more than wide awake, from the growing suspense. "How did I not see that she's grown this...ill?" Joe thought to himself. It had made him sad. He and his mother were close, but he now realized that they were nowhere near close enough.

"I guess that's not too surprising. Not noticing, that is. Many people overlook the faults of their loved ones. They usually just dismiss oddities, as eccentricities. But this, goes beyond merely that" Joe thought to himself, as his anxious thoughts marched onward.

If she had really fallen to this shaky of a mental state, then he had not been paying close enough attention. "To think we'd really want to cook and eat a crocodil..." he thought, groaning, in agitation. Gulping, the man now prepared to broach the dreaded subject.

"Okay, let's get this show on the road" the grandmother had shouted from her bedroom. "Sounds like she's changed her shirt" Joe thought.

"How am I going to talk to her about this? What would Dr. Boltzmann do in this situation?" he mutters under his breath, thinking of his psychiatrist. "It's too bad he's not here right now. I would like to hear his advice. Or on second thought, maybe not. He might have her committed then" Joe thought.

"No, that's not possible. They don't really commit people anymore..." he continued thinking. "I wonder if having the same type of medication, I take, could help her cope better" Joe wondered. "She's my mother, and we have the same genes, so it makes sense that it could work. I mean, it does make me feel better..." he thought as he pulled his prescription bottle out of his pocket, now looking at it. "I wonder...maybe I should offer her some of my pills to see if it helps her at all. I know she's old, and you typically need a script from a doctor for this kind of thing, but..."

"Alright, now where's everyone else? I don't know about you, but I'm famished..." his mother says, as she re-enters the kitchen. "I can't believe what you've done here" Joe, says to his mother sternly. "What? What did I do?", she remarks, seeing that her son is upset. "For the love of God, Mom...Jimmy and Rafe are here. Do you really think that's something they need to see?" he asked her softly, trying not to let his sons hear the matter they're discussing.

"I'm afraid I really don't know what you're

talking about, Joe. What do you mean? Something they need to see?" She says. "No!" Joe says, stopping himself once he realized he had spoken too loudly. "No", he whispers softly. "No. Something, they don't need to see. Why can't this just be a normal breakfast? A normal visit? God know's it hasn't been an easy past year for all of us. Don't you think this would only stir things up? Bring back bad memories?"

Eve pauses, as she attempts to piece together what Joe was trying to say to her. "Am, I finally getting across?" her son asked her. "Joe, I really have no idea what you're saying here." Now growing visibly upset, Joe grows more concerned. "For the love of God, do you honestly not see a problem with this?" he says pointing to the oven. Were you really going to try to feed them that?" Joe says as he grabs a pair of oven mitts.

"It seems there's been a huge misunderstanding here, Joe" remarks his mother. " Oh yes, there has been" Joe says in a sarcastic manner, as he places the oven mitts on his hands preparing himself. He glances over, at the oven, "I don't even want to see it at this point" the man thought to himself. "It's just too morbid."

"Is the duck almost ready?" asks Jimmy. Surprised, Joe swiftly turns around to find that the boy had come back in the room in the middle of their quarreling. "The...duck?" Joe stutters and blushes. "Yes. The duck. Why? What did you think it was?" Grandma Eve asks her son. "Nothing...never mind" Joe says, turning around to shield his now red face.

"Wait a minute" she says thinking to herself. "Oh my God, did you think that I...?" She responds, at last realizing what the confusion was about. Smiling, she scoffs at the suggestion. She then clears her throat in relief. "I know I'm old, but I'm not completely senile. Not insane. I can't believe you would think I'd do such a thing."

"S-Sorry. Yeah, it was stupid" Joe says, now feeling like a complete fool. "Can we at least eat now?" she asks her son, again. "Or are there any other crazy things you're worried I'm up to?" She says frustrated. "Look, I said I'm sorry, Mom. Okay, let's eat. Jimmy, help us set up the table, okay?" "Alright, Dad" replied the young man. The boy walked over to the kitchen table while he carried a large pile of dishes and eating utensils. "Dad, you already made the table. Did you forget?" Jimmy says. "What? No, I didn't" Joe looks over at the table and discovers that it is indeed as his son claimed. "I didn't make it. Did your brother? I thought he was still in his room?" Joe
states.

"I dunno..." Jimmy replied. "It doesn't really matter. Just go find him, and bring him back, so we can get going, after we eat" Joe says. "You mean we can't stay any longer?", Jimmy asks frowning. "Well, you guys still have homework to finish up. I guess you can do it here. But you've missed enough classes this year, I can't let you miss any more" Joe tells his son. "Yeah, okay" Jimmy says, as he walks off to find his brother.

Chapter 14: Halloween Forever

"Hey Rafe, Breakfast is ready!" Jimmy, yells. "Don't just shout out. You're not playing hide and seek now. Just go to his room and fetch him" Joe instructs of his son. Jimmy approaches Rafe's bedroom and encounters an unexpected sight.

The door to Rafe's room, only a few feet away had abruptly slammed shut. "Rafe?" Jimmy calls out, once more. "Was Rafe getting dressed and closed the door for privacy?" the boy wondered. Jimmy, didn't know, but the way the door had slammed closed so quickly, unnerved him. "I need to stop being such a wimp. It's nothing" thought the young man. "I'm just being paranoid because of that nightmare I had. That's all it is" the boy consoled himself.

"C'mon, food's ready" Jimmy said, with his brother's bedroom door in front of him. No reply. The boy proceeded to try knocking on the door. Still nothing. "Rafe? Didn't you hear me?", Jimmy says, as he grabs the doors handle.

"What's this?" remarks Jimmy while he wiggles the handle. "Locked" he says to himself. "Come on Rafe. You know Dad says we shouldn't lock doors." Just as he finished that word, he remembered his journey from the night before. His memory was still fuzzy, but pieces of it were beginning to come back. The boy remembered all the doors he went through, and the grotesque tunnels he had to traverse.

"That...that was only a dream" The boy tells himself. "Hey Dad, the door's locked", Jimmy says as he walks back to the kitchen. "Dad? Grandma?" Jimmy looks around the room. "Now, where did they go off to?" the boy thought. It would seem that both his father and grandmother had left the kitchen.

"They know better than to leave the oven on" Jimmy thinks, as he approaches the oven and reaches over to its switches. Just as the boy was about to turn the oven off, a loud banging thud came from the oven, itself. "Woah. What was that?" Jimmy said, as he turned on the oven light.

Crouching down, the child peek's inside the oven. "Still too dark to make it out" the boy observes, as he hears another crashing sound in the distance. "Rafe?" It had come from across the room he was just at. Rafe's bedroom. "Did you break something!?" Jimmy shouts out.

"This is just too much. That dream was bad enough, and now...I only just got up. I'm still tired." Jimmy muttered to himself. "That noise? It sounded like glass shattering", the boy thought. Thunder begins to rumble, as another storm sets in. The young man, glances outside of the kitchen window. "I don't remember rain being in the forecast" he thinks, growing annoyed. "I don't feel like going outside in the rain, today", Jimmy thinks, as he quickly turns off the oven. "I'll worry about that later. I gotta make sure Rafe is up, first" the boy remarks, beginning to open several drawers in the kitchen.

"Maybe this'll work" he says pulling out a pair of scissors with thin long blades. The boy walks over to Rafe's door again and sticks one of the thin scissor blades in the keyhole. A popping noise is heard, as Jimmy exclaims "Yes!" in elation, realizing he had successfully picked the door lock.

Jimmy pulls out the scissors, and the door creaks open a few inches. "Freaky. Why did it do that?" He pondered, growing anxious. "Rafe?" Jimmy softly said as he leaned his head near the crack in the door. The boys eyes peered into the dark room. "You still asleep?" Jimmy asked. The lights were still off, but there was a dim glimmer of light in the room from one of the drawn curtains. "I guess that means he's up?" Jimmy wonders as he slowly began to set foot in the room.

"Alright, I'm coming in now" Jimmy says, with his eyes surveying the bedroom's entrance. Looking toward the bed, he notices that the sheets are tossed halfway hanging off of the mattress. "Yeah, he's up. Like usual, he didn't even bother to make his bed" Jimmy observes. Approaching his brother's bed, the boy hears a jingling noise. "Hmm?" Jimmy mumbles to himself, as he reacted to the sound. The boy looks at the foot of the bed and sees a large chandelier. It sat in broken pieces, as the room's fan gently blew down at it, causing a jingling noise.

Chills come across the boy, as he thinks back to the day before. About his father explaining the story of The Phantom of the Opera to him, and of the chandelier in the tale. "Reminds me of the stuff Dad was talking about in the car" he mutters. Jimmy turns his attention to the bathroom door connected to the bedroom. It's door was slightly opened. "Rafe? Are you in there?" Jimmy asks yet again, his heart now thumping heavily in an uneasy rhythm. Walking up to the door, the boy calls out one final time. "Rafe?" The young man enters the dark bathroom, switching on its light by the side entrance.

It's only a few moments after he turns on the light that the pandemonium happens. Jimmy gasps, seeing that the mirror above the bathroom sink, had been shattered. Pieces of glass remain at his feet, aside the base of the sink. "What happened in here?" Jimmy thinks to himself, as he quickly paces his head back and forth trying to figure out what had transpired.

"Get out of there, right now" gargled a disembodied voice. "Where did that come from?" wondered the boy. He was unable to detect it's origin. The voice had seemed to echo all throughout the entirety of the household in a seemingly omnipresent manner. "Was that my dad?" Frightened, the boy quickly bolts back toward the door, only to find it locked again.

"I don't remember locking this" Jimmy thought, as he reached into his pocket pulling out the scissors again when he noticed a faint burning smell in the distance. "Is that from the stove?" he initially thought, since that would naturally be the assumption of most people, especially considering his father and grandmother were preparing breakfast.

Red lights begin to flash on a device near the top of the room. Moments later, the same contraption, sounded an alarm blast indicating some kind of grave danger. "The fire alarm", the boy thought. Just as he was about to pick the door's lock with the scissor blade, yet again, Jimmy heard another sound in the distance. A sound, not from any alarm this time, but rather a voice. A voice, which made him realize he was in danger far greater than any alarm could indicate.

"I'm coming for you!" shouts a grim voice, turning Jimmy's blood to ice. "What on earth is happening?" the boy thought, in horror. A rumbling sensation began rocking the floor of the house. It sounded like a stampede of wild beasts. "Was that coming from whoever made that voice, just now?" he thought to himself. The boy stares in blank bewilderment as orange smoke began creeping under the doorway. "Whatever this is, it isn't coming from the stove" Jimmy observed.

Knowing he can't go through the door now, the boy turned around and looked for a place to hide. "Wait, a second. No, I can't hide. What am I thinking? I need to get out. The alarms are going off, so if there really is a fire then I can't just stay here..." He began frantically pleading for help in his mind. With no explanation, the lights dim in the house, leaving no illumination other than the red glowing flashes of the alarm.

"What's going on? What's happening?" Jimmy thought, as the young man began to panic. It was at this moment, that he began growing very confused and frustrated, that he was unable to shed any light whatsoever on the situation. "I know you're in there" yells a menacing voice from beyond the door. "Who's that?" Jimmy, asks. The boy receives cackling laughter, in response.

Jimmy's heart sank, "Grandma...Dad..." he thought. "They're, in there with whoever that is. I have to go back!" the boy thought to himself. The boy, began shaking, fearing for the safety of his family, and of his self.

"No, I can't" Jimmy realized. "My brother, too. He's not in here. He must still be out there, too. Isn't he?" Jimmy said to himself. "Damn it. I can't right now. I can't go out there. It's just too risky", he thought as he put the pair of scissors back into his pocket. Frustrated, Jimmy recognized the reality of the situation. As difficult as it appeared to be, it didn't seem like he had much of a choice at the moment. Going back, would indeed be too dangerous, for him to attempt.

"Alright. The window, then" Jimmy thinks as he ran over to the only window in the room. "Good. It's not locked" he says as he notices the latch on the window hasn't been pulled down. An uneasy stillness fills the room. The young man had felt as if he were in the calm of a storm, or the eye of a tornado.

"The alarms? They stopped?" Jimmy, thought. "Maybe Rafe and Dad are already outside" he hoped. "Enough's enough" Jimmy told himself in a stern manner, as he attempted to muster up courage. "I'm getting out of here, now. "Astonished by the course of events, Jimmy takes a deep breath, as if going underwater and climbs up toward the opened window.

"This doesn't feel right" Jimmy thought. "I need to go. Everything's going to be alright" the frightened boy told himself as he opened the window and entered. He had feigned bravery, but he was still worried.

The boy shakes his body, as he pulls his weight through the window. "Alright. I'm outside, now" Jimmy said. He was concerned he would not fit through, for a moment. "It looks like I'm in the woods?" Jimmy observed he as he peered around the dark forested enigma.

"What? T-This place? This isn't her backyard" he said, baffled. It was as if his grandmother had a secret garden, only accessible through the window. "Why is this here?" Jimmy thinks as he looks in the distance. "I remember this. I saw this in my dream" Jimmy thought, as he looked down toward the forested terrain.

He could see a treehouse in the distance. A feeling of doom, shot down, deep within the boy. Jimmy quivered, and his face formed a sad expression of someone who had been dealt a great loss. "Why is this happening to me?" Jimmy lamented, with tears quickly welling up with eyes.

The young man was confused and disturbed by the nightmarish chain of events. Breathing slowly to steady his racing heart-rate, Jimmy slowly regains his composure and turns his attention toward the entrance of the treehouse. "Another sign?" Jimmy said, perplexed. "It says...Welcome?" the boy said as he read it. "God, if you're listening... I'm really scared" Jimmy prayed silently. His prayers, were cut off prematurely, by a slamming sound from inside the house he had just escaped from.

"Oh, no. I could be seen through the window. He observed and turned around toward the treehouse. "Dad, Rafe, Grandma, please be alright" the boy hopelessly prayed, as he neared the only possible hiding place in his range of sight. The treehouse.

A dim orange glow suddenly begins to emit from inside the treehouse. Jimmy's heart pounds, as he turns around and nears the door. "Maybe they're already in here?" Jimmy wonders to himself, with his hand gently opening the wooden door.

"There's nobody here?" Jimmy remarks, as he attempts to make sense of his surroundings. Just as it had looked from outside, the place he had entered, was some kind of children's treehouse. "Had Grandma had this treehouse and garden all along? Why keep it a secret?" the boy wondered, contemplating the mystery. Jimmy approaches a small table with an eerie game-board, on it. "A Ouija board?" the boy says as he observes the objcct on the table. "Yes, No, Hello, Goodbye" the words on the Ouija board read, alongside the alphabet and numbers 1 through 9. At the corners of the board, were illustrations of the sun and moon. A large sealed container of what he presumed to be water, resided on the table along with it.

Deep in thought, the boy squints, as he notices another sheet of paper on the table. On the paper, was a crudely drawn illustration of a face. "This, drawing...this face...." Jimmy mutters under his breath.

To the side of the table, stood a chair placed right in the center of the room. The way it had been arranged, made it's placement almost look as if it were some kind of throne. The chair had yet another note on it. "Sit here at exactly midnight" the note read on top of its cushioned seat.

"This note..." Jimmy thought, as he examined the note's directions. "It's written in bright colors. Was this written with crayons?" he wondered to himself. On top of the wall directly behind the chair, remained a clock. It looked like one of those creepy cat clocks, where it's eyes move back and forth. It's eyes, moving in unison with its tail. Except, instead of a cat, this clock was made to look like a crocodile.

The boy leaned in closer, looking at the time on the clock. 11:55pm. "But I just got up a little while ago. It shouldn't be night-time" Jimmy thought to himself, growing more confused than ever. But yes, it was almost midnight. At least, according to the clock. It was dark outside, too. "Could that be just because of the storm? Or is it actually night, now?" Jimmy began questioning his reality.

Looking at the clock, the young man saw that there were only just a few more minutes before midnight. It was as if he arrived here at precisely the right moment. As if he were fated to do so. Like some unseen force, was guiding his journey.

With his heart beating rapidly, Jimmy glanced over at the clock again. "Well, I guess it's time" he thought, as he gulped. Jimmy walked over to the chair, not knowing what to expect. He breathed a sharp breath in anticipation of the unknown and sat down. The clock struck midnight and continued ticking away.

Chapter 15:
The Boy with Green Eyes

"Now here's the part where things get really weird" remarks a boy with crocodile green eyes, as he holds a flashlight to his face. The reflecting light, making his eyes look like that of a nocturnal animal in the darkness. "Ha-ha, what? That sounds crazy, Pete" a youthful voice exclaims to him. "I'm telling you, it's true. They really did it, Mark" proclaimed Pcte.

A third voice chimed in, "I don't know. It seems super far-fetched. Seems childish to believe it..." "Well, we are children still, right?" Pete, the boy with green eyes remarks. "This is getting too spooky, I'm turning the lights back on", says a voice as a flash of light illuminated the room.

Three young children sat around a table inside a wooded treehouse. "Halloween is coming up. We could try it ourselves" Pete said. "You might want to explain it again, so Johnny understands, too. He only just got here" replied Mark, as he pointed to another boy who was slightly younger than the other two.

Pete, let out an annoyed grunt. "Alright, Mark. I'll give you guys the tedious exposition again" he said, as the youngest boy leaned in closer, eager to his what his two friends were bickering about for so long. "Okay, you can start the story, Pete" "Ok, I will. But make sure you pay close attention to what

I'm saying here. It's not like reality is like a book you can just flip back to and re-read parts you overlooked. Do you understand what I'm saying? Follow my words closely...." the boy with green eyes responded, holding the flashlight to his face.

"People say there was some experiment a long time ago. At least a few decades ago, I think" Pete began. "It was an experiment done by some scientists who tried to see if they could communicate with ghosts" he said. "Not just any ghosts though. Made up ghosts" Mark said jumping in. "Aren't all ghosts made up, though?" Johnny the younger boy asks. "Well, what he means is fictional people" Pete said, realizing that Johnny was only growing increasingly confused by his unsatisfactory explanation.

"Let me put it this way" Pete began to say, stopping momentarily to think about his words closely. "These scientists got together in a room, and they came up with all the traits of a person they were making up. Their name, birthday, things they liked, and didn't like, and other stuff. Do you follow so far?" Pete asked looking over at Johnny. "Uh. I think so?" Johnny replied, with feigned certainty.

"So, they made up a person. I don't remember their name, but that part doesn't matter for us. Because if we end up doing it, we'll need to make up a name, ourselves. Anyway, these scientists, gave their character a story so detailed, that they were supposed to have created results in real life" Pete continued.

"What do you mean by that?" Johnny asked Pete. "Well, it's a theory about how if enough people think about something, even if it's not real, they can make it a reality. I know it sounds hard to believe, but they say it happened" Pete said with conviction in his breath. "Those are just tall tales" Mark said, mockingly. "Urban legends, stories to tell around the campfire and such" Mark continued to say, in a dismissive manner. Irked by Mark's cynicism, Pete shoot's his friend and annoyed grimace, which causes Mark to grin. Mark's attitude had managed to get under Pete skin, and it amused him, in an odd way.

"You're a skeptic about everything, Mark. How about we just try it out ourselves then? What's the worst that could happen?" Pete suggested. "Well, it sounds kind of creepy you guys. Kind of Satanic or something" Johnny said uneasily.

"Then I guess that makes it perfect for Halloween. But, alright. I'll play along. Let's do it up here, to make it even creepier" Mark said. "In our treehouse? Yeah, sure why not. I guess it makes for a good place. We've told ghost stories here before, anyway. So, I suppose that would just be natural" Pete responded.

"What are you doing?" Mark asks as Pete pulls out a notebook, and places it on the table. "If we're

139

going to do this, then let's make sure we do it all right. First thing's first. We should make a list" Pete says as he opens the notebook to a blank page and grasps a ballpoint pen firmly in his hand.

"A list? Ah, I get it. Like from the old experiment you were talking about. Okay, but where do we even start?" Johnny asks. "I guess at the beginning. What should our character's name be?" Mark inquires.

Pete looks over to his side at a small caged vivarium he had placed on the table inside the treehouse. A small snake slithers about the cage, wiggling through the rocks and sand inside its home. The other two boys notice Pete looking at the vivarium, and of his pet inside.

"Huh? You wannna name him after your snake?" Mark says, surprised. "Well, I don't see any reason why we can't do that" Johnny says, as Pete begins to write in the notebook. The boys continue to detail the fictitious characters life in meticulous detail, growing immersed in their own creativity. Their imaginations run wild, as the hours go by, and Johnny notices the ticking of the clock in the room.

"You guys, it's getting kinda late" Johnny says. "Yeah, I guess we should get heading back home. I can't believe we're really going to do this. So, we're meeting up on Halloween for this, then?" Mark asks. The boys both nod, affirming they're all in agreement, and they part ways for the evening.

Pete grabs the notes, and the tank on the table, containing his pet, and he looks out of the treehouse window, toward a house. A woman, waves at him, through the window of the home, and Pete smirks, waving back. "I'll be there in a second, Mom!" the boy yells through the treehouse window, leaning his body halfway through it. It Pete's mother, April. Packing up, he leaves his backyard and returns home.

Going directly to his room, the boy dims the light, and rests his head on his pillow, while the day's events raced through his mind. "Make a made up person real"? It was as Mark had put it. "Crazy" he thought. It sounded impossible, but they were going to try it. The boy continued thinking about the matter, as he slowly started falling asleep as the autumn night came to pass.

Days fly off the calendar as October nears its end. Halloween approaches, and the boys had all almost forgotten about their pact, were it not for Pete who called his friends the night before. "So, we're still doing it?" Pete asks holding a bulky land-line phone to his ear. "Doing? What?" Johnny asked, forgetful. Mark had asked the same thing. "Doing what?" Hearing this, irritated Pete. If it were not for him, how would anything they arranged ever get done?" Pete thought privately. "What would they do, without me?"

"Oh, that. I totally forgot!" Johnny said, so

loudly, Pete almost dropped his phone. "You guys are really weird. You sure you want to do that, still?" the boy asked, while secretly wishing now that Pete had forgotten like Mark had. Or that Pete at least had second thoughts and changed his mind.

The truth was it really did freak Johnny out. Not just their plan, but the whole idea. He disliked meta-fictional topics, as it unsettled him. The topic forced the boy to think about his own existence. That was something Johnny did not like to do. He wasn't sure how anyone even could. He had heard that some of the greatest scientific minds, had driven themselves to madness, thinking about such ideas. Questions like "How is existence even possible?"

"Yeah, why wouldn't I? It sounds like a fun experiment, even if it doesn't work. Why? You're not afraid or anything, are you?" Pete asked. "No, of course not" Johnny lied. The boy did not want to reveal his true feelings about their game. Pete didn't normally poke fun of him as much as Mark liked to, but he still didn't want to give the impression that he was a chicken.

Being that Johnny was younger than both Mark and Pete, Johnny felt that he perhaps had to prove his courage to them, and other older kids, from time to time. Even if he said he didn't like thinking about that kind of stuff, they might still try to joke about him. Johnny wasn't necessarily an insecure child, but the young man didn't want to get embarrassed by his friends.

"You still have all the notes and everything, then?" Johnny asked. "Yeah. I have it all right here with me" Pete said. "So, after trick or treating we'll meet up, right?" inquired Johnny. "That's right. Before midnight, at the treehouse. We'll still need some time to get things ready, though. We can take care of anything we need to add to our story during lunch at school. Later in the day, let's meet up no later than an hour before midnight. That is, if that works for you" Pete inquired. "Ok, that sounds good. So, at 11, then?" Johnny said. "Yeah, at 11, sharp" Pete responded.

"That's pretty late. But I guess it's Halloween, so my parents will probably make an exception, and let me stay out with you guys till then" Johnny said to his friend. "Cool. See you then" Pete told him as he hung up the phone, leaving nothing but the dial tone beeping, in thunderous repetition. "Who are you talking to, Pete?" chimed a maternal voice. Nobody, Mom" Pete says back, looking over his shoulder. "This should be fun" Pete thought to himself. Unlike his Johnny, he was very much looking forward to the event.

Chapter 16: Basilisk

"Yeah, I understand it, but it sounds as far-fetched as your game, Pete" Mark says as he Johnny, and Pete sit at a crowded lunchroom table. "So, if someone is struck by lightning, their atoms can be rearranged again, if lightning strikes, again?" Johnny asks.

"We were talking about it in science class. About quantum mechanics, and how anything is possible. There's even a theory about how a human brain can pop up anywhere in the universe, with full memories created intact" Pete, says. "What's the theory called?" Johnny inquires. "If I remember correctly, I think it's called a Boltzmann Brain. That's what the argument is called, that is" Pete responds.

"Is there a reason for that name, anyway?" Mark asks. "Probably a name of some scientist, who had something to do with the idea" Pete says, uncertain as to its origin. "Well, whoever came up with it, must've been totally off his rocker" Mark scoffs. "Hey, since we're doing these last minute tune-up's to our characters, we still haven't decided on a name for our doctor, right? That sounds like a good doctor name. What do you guys think? " Johnny suggests, looking at his friends for their approval.

Shrugging his shoulders, Mark sneer's at his

friend and crosses his arms. "What the hell are you asking me for, Johnny? I'm just going along with Pete's game..." "Sure, Johnny nice idea" Pete says, noticing Johnny's discouraged demeaner after Mark's negative answer.

"Chill out, Mark. Johnny's just trying to help. Don't be such a dick" Pete, chastised him. Pete liked Mark, but the brutally honest truth was that the guy really could be a demeaning asshole, sometimes. He was used to tolerating his cantankerous temperament, since he's known him for several years, but Johnny met him this year.

Mark and Pete's relationship was almost like a platonic version of an old married couple, with the amount of time they bickered amongst one another. Two people, who often were diametrically opposed, in numerous instances. Yet they endured one another's faults, because they've always been close, and probably always would be. Like a captain going down with his sinking ship, who see's things to the bitter end.

"Anyway, this barely counts as science, Pete" Mark tells him. "Yeah, it sounds pretty flimsy. Why were you guys talking about this stuff in science class?" Johnny asks squinting his eyes, in a confused manner. "I thought you guys were studying biology."

"Well, it's about atoms at stuff. So, it's at least sort of relevant to the subjects we study. We had just finished a test, and I guess the teacher was just kind of trying to fill time till the bell rang. It's Halloween, so we had begun talking about creepy theoretical ideas" Pete responds as he opens a milk carton. "Well, what about our experiment? Did you ask everyone what they thought about that?" Johnny asks, as the boy takes a bite out of his sandwich.

"I did. But I didn't tell them that we're actually trying it. Since we're at a religious school and everything, they would probably overreact, and get paranoid if I mentioned that we're going to use a Ouija board for it" Pete tells him. "What did they have to say? Anything interesting?" Johnny asks his friend.

"Nothing that was really that helpful. The teacher seemed to think it was a cool idea and everything, but that it wasn't very practical, when it comes down to it. That maybe it would work for part of a scary story to tell, but that the premise simply wasn't possible" Pete answers. "Because it's not. How would something like that even be possible to test? It's not scientific, unless you can demonstrate something, you idiot" Mark says bitterly, as he hastily gulps down his soda.

"Some of the other kids said it reminded them of some urban legends though. Apparently, there's something called a Tulpa. I didn't know about it before, but it's a made up person you can make, too" Pete says. "That was some sort of a Buddhist

146

concept. Then there's something called a Basilisk" Pete says, taking a break to sip some of his milk. "Basi-what?" Johnny asks.

"Basilisk. It means some kind of snake, but the name's just figurative. At least in the context they were discussing. Anyway, it's an urban legend, about how a fictional monster, demon or whatever can become real. How it can make people create it's existence" Pete explains to him.

"How's it do that?" Johnny asks, leaning his chair in, closer toward the lunchroom table. Moving the chair, Johnny had accidentally caused it to make a loud screeching noise against the floor. It was a quick and loud screech, like an unexpected strike of lightning, or nails on a classroom chalkboard.

"Sorry" Johnny says, noticing Mark covering his ears, with an annoyed expression on his face. "Can't I even eat lunch in peace?" Mark says. "I said I'm sorry, didn't I? Anyway, go on, Pete. I'm listening" Johnny says to his friends, growing more curious by the minute, by the explanation.

"Well, think of it this way. Let's say that a group of people participate in the creation of a monster, because if they don't help make it, the monster will make them suffer in the future. Once it exists for real, that is. That it can create an incentive for forcing or tricking people in doing so. Maybe it can even promise to reward them, if they help bring upon its creation" Pete tells him. Putting his arm on the table, and resting his chin on his palm, Johnny asks "Not that I'm convinced that's this is possible, but if it is, then how do we know that's not what we're doing?" Johnny says, sounding concerned.

"Don't worry, that can't be the case. We wrote all of our characters as nice, didn't we?" Pete says dismissively. "You guys are already putting too much thought and effort into this crazy game" Mark says shaking his head. "Yeah, I guess so" Johnny replies with a chuckle.

"It's the same kind of nonsense they were talking about in philosophy class, too. What was that term...self something..." Mark says, scratching his head. "Self-Cognition" Pete answers. "What's that mean?" Johnny asks. "Something about being aware you're observing yourself, and the philosophical implications. Just stupid shit, that only sounds smart" Mark scoffs.

"You're being a bit hasty, Mark. It's a little more complex than that. It deals with heightened awareness about the true reality of things. About how you can reach Nirvana or whatever you want to call it. How a sudden act of self realization, can tap into a hidden grand power. A sort of revalation, I guess, through your own consciousness " Pete says. "That sounds like the most pretentious bullshit in the world, to me" Mark says.

"Okay, only one deep subject at a time, you guys...so the urban legends you were talking about though....where did these kids even hear about these urban legends?" Johnny asks his friends. "I think some of them read about the stuff online. Probably message boards, or internet forums. You know, where a bunch of crazy people talk about paranormal things. Sounds reliable to me" Mark says, rolling his eyes. "I don't think our teacher liked the direction where our conversation was going. It was just derailing into crazy talk. He started telling us to get out bags ready, and before we knew it, that was the end of the discussion in our class. The bell rang, and that was that" Mark responds to him.

"Speaking of which, we should probably get ready" Mark says looking at the clock in the lunchroom. "Yeah, okay" Pete says, as he finishes his milk. Beginning to clear the table, Pete turns to his friends. "Don't forget. Tonight's the night, we try it out" he tells the two. The lunchroom bell rings, and the three boys, along with all the other students in the lunchroom begin to clear out. "Yeah, I know, Pete" Mark says. "Don't worry, I'll be there, too" Johnny says waving bye to his friends, as they all part their separate ways for the day.

Chapter 17: Halloween's End

All Hallows' Eve had finally come, as the trio of boys assembled in the dark of the night. Pete had arrived first and patiently waited for the other two boys. "What's in the bag?" asked Mark as he arrived. "Don't you remember? The stuff we needed to bring to make the character we had planned out" Pete answered. "Oh, right. You're really taking this thing very seriously, aren't you?" Mark responded.

"I'm on time, right?" Johnny asked, emerging from the shadows of the breezy autumn night. "Yeah, you're on time. But we don't have much time left to spare. Let's go inside, and get started on this" Pete said, as the three of them climbed up into the treehouse.

"Good, you brought the board" Pete said, looking at a black cardboard box Johnny was holding. "Yeah. It's here" the boy replied. Pete smiled. "Nice costumes, by the way. Just like we planned in our story" Pete says to his friends. "Thanks. Yours is neat, too" Johnny replied. The three of them were indeed all still wearing their Halloween costumes they had worn trick or treating. Pete as Peter Pan, Johnny as Sherlock Holmes, and Mark as the Phantom of the Opera.

"Why did I have to be Peter Pan though? Just because of my name? That's a little too on the nose, don't you think? If you ask me, I think it would have made more sense for Johnny to wear it, since he's the youngest" Pete said, as he observed the other boys costumes.

"Because you're the smallest. Besides, they match your eyes, and there's no way I'm wearing green tights. This was all your idea, just be glad we're going along with your stupid game, Pete", Mark said. "It's a tunic, and no one forced you to do this. Besides, you helped us come up with the ideas, Mark. Anyway, let's go. Bring the board, Johnny" Pete said, pointing to Johnny's box.

"My older brother told me to be careful with these things though" Johnny said. "Don't worry about that. Ouija boards are just kids toys" Mark said to Johnny. "I mean, unless Milton Bradley, is actually a front run by Satan, I don't think we'll have anything to worry about" Mark said in a sarcastic tone, as the three of them climb up a ladder leading into the treehouse.

"Well, all the same, we have this in case anything really does go wrong" Pete says as he places a large sealed bottle on a table. "What's in there?" Johnny asks. "Holy water" Pete replies, as Mark shakes his head in mortification. "Now this is just silly" Mark says, holding back a laugh.

The three boys placed the box on the table and opened it up. "Cool, it glows in the dark" Mark said, as he observed the glowing board. "Yeah. Let's turn the lights on, in here though. At least while we get things set up" Pete said, as he switched the light on a lantern, he had brought inside with them.

Next, Pete proceeded to pull a notebook out of his bag. He quickly flipped through the pages inside of it, making sure everything seemed to be in order and then placed it aside the Ouija board on the table. "All the pages seem to be here" Pete said, as he closed the notebook. Even the drawing of that one character's face we made.

"It seems like overkill. Why did we have to write so much? I mean, we even made up all of these other people, just for one character" said Mark. "A fictional version of you, too. Except you're dead, in the story. That was a pretty morbid and meta thing to write about. Plus, that therapist, and minister" replied Johnny. "Psychiatrist and priest, but yeah" said Pete.

"It's just so the details of their lives are as fully fleshed out as we can possibly make them. It shouldn't matter, just as long as we're all on the same page and know our character's history. Even if we went into more detail than needed, it's better safe than sorry, right?" Pete responds to Johnny, as the three of them bring their seats to the table, as they begin their preparations.

"Why make their lives so depressing? A dead kid, a monster after them. Plus, that poor dad" Johnny said. "Well, it's supposed to give the characters an incentive. A drive to succeed" Pete answered.

"What about writing yourself into it, Pete? That's pretty meta. I don't know about you, but it sure made me uncomfortable. You're my friend, and I don't want to think of you as dead. Was there a reason you wrote about yourself like that?" Johnny asks him.

"A reason for why I came up with the idea of me being dead? No, not really. At least, not exactly. There was no real reason. It's just the way it happened as our ideas progressed. I saw a story on the news about a kid who got killed by a crocodile" Pete said, as he began adjusting the Ouija board's placement on the table.

"Hmm, or maybe it was an alligator? I don't remember, but I guess that part's irrelevant. Anyway, that's what gave me the initial idea. When I first heard about it, I thought it would be a good premise to use for a story, since it was such a creepy and horrible thing to happen. I didn't think I would go this far with it, though. Since I never planned on doing this till, we all started talking about our little experiment. As for why I wrote about myself with a fictional family...I don't know. I guess it's because I always wished I had brothers, and never really got to know my father" Pete said to Johnny.

"So, there's actually science behind this?" skeptical, Mark furrowed his brow "Do you remember at the beginning of the school year, that stuff about observation? You know, in science class?" Pete asked. "I remember, but I'm just not sure I buy into that stuff. Johnny's not in our class, so he probably doesn't know about that part, Pete."

"Oh, right. Sorry, Johnny. Basically, it's about the way people observe things. That their perception, can actually generate results. Like with particles and stuff. It's complicated science, and not something I'm an expert on or anything. But according to what I remember, atoms react differently to experiments if they're being looked at by people. Or at least, something kinda like that" Pete said. He was unsure of the science behind it, himself.

"That's weird. How can that be?" Johnny asked. "I dunno. But that experiment I was talking about before, was based on similar ideas and tests. About how there's more to our own consciousness than we may realize" Pete told the boy. Johnny was skeptical, too. Although, his curiosity was growing by the minute, despite the uneasiness he felt.

"This experiment...the one you can't remember the name of, Pete...these tests... were actually done by scientists? By adults?" Johnny asked. "Yes, but not just ordinary adults. Very smart ones. Like people with high IQ's and people who were supposed to have clairvoyance and stuff." Pete said. "Clair-what? Johnny asked, unfamiliar with the term Pete had used. "Like psychic powers. Fortune tellers able to read minds. Paranormal stuff, ya know? Those type of things" Pete answered. "Oh, okay" Johnny replied, still wary of the general idea, and of what they could be getting themselves into.

"How could such a large group of so called intelligent people, conduct such an experiment? They must've been out of their minds" Mark said. "Why would we have any more success than they did, anyway? I mean, just look at us. We're so young" Mark said. "That part makes sense to me. It's because we're kids, right? Because of our imagination?" Johnny said, in an upbeat tone.

"I don't know, Pete. We didn't fully flesh things out. Yes, it's detailed, but I think it could use some more work. I know you guys think it's a lot, but we did some of it in kind of in a rush. We made very detailed parts about the insignificant stuff." "That doesn't matter, Mark. It only matters for our character, anyway" Pete, said to him.

"But we have several characters, Pete" Johnny responds. "You know the one I mean. Besides, what's wrong with that?" Pete asks. "Well, you said when this was done in the past, it was just with one character, right?" Johnny asks, concerned. "Yes, that's right. It's never been done like this. Not till tonight, that is. Johnny, Mark, you guys just need to have faith in your imagination."

"Woah, that's really creepy, guys" Mark said as Pete pulled an object resembling a human face from out of his backpack. "Is that a mask?" Johnny asks, holding a lantern closer to the strange object. "No, Johnny. It's the head of one of those CPR test-dummies." "Why do you even have one of those, Pete?" Mark asked, as he leaned in close inspecting its deformed looking face. "Gross, it already kind of feels like a person's face, too" Mark observes as the boy presses his index finger at the center of the face. "Don't poke it, Mark. These are supposed to be expensive, I think" Pete instructs of his friend, worried he might damage it.

"Anyway, I found one around my house, I think it was from one of my mom's lifeguard classes." Pete placed the eerie plastic head on a chair in the middle of the room. "Let's see, now. Next, we're going to need to attach its body and legs" Pete said, as he took out a large sweatshirt and pair of sweatpants from his backpack. "These will do" Pete stated, as he proceeded to open up a large yard waste bag at his side.

"What's in there?" Johnny asks. "Take a look" Pete says as he shakes the bag, packing its contents tightly. Johnny and Mark stand out of their chairs, and lean toward the opened bag, revealing it to be filled with leaves.

"I filled this bag up, when I was raking the leaves earlier. We can use these leaves for its guts. You know, to help form what's supposed to be its body" Pete said as the three of them assembled the body of their fictitious character and placed it on the chair. "Here, use these sticks. Put them inside, to hold it up. That way, it won't fall apart. It'll be like its skeleton. That also makes it fitting for the season, don't you guys think? For Halloween, that is" Pete said.

"Looks like a scarecrow" Johnny said, as the three of them observed their creation from across the treehouse. They placed their creation in a chair across from the table with the Ouija board. The sticks inside of it, propped it up, and gave it the appearance of having arms and legs. "It kind of looks like it's sitting on a throne" Johnny observes.

"Do you realize how stupid this looks, Pete? That were trying to make a makeshift dummy come to life like Frankenstein? This isn't some kind of silly movie. We're not even doing this for a class, or anything. Seems pointless. God, I can't believe you already mentioned that we're doing this in class. They'd laugh their asses off, if they knew the entirety of this crazy idea."

"Wait! He's missing one thing" The other two boys looked at Johnny with anticipation. Johnny, had paused, as if he were reluctant to continue his observation. "Well, what is it? Don't just leave us in suspense" Pete said. "Yeah, out with it. Don't leave us hanging" Mark said, agreeing with Pete. "His soul" Johnny said, as he pulled out a scrap of unused paper from the notebook and placed it on the table. "What do you intend for us to do? Just write Soul on this paper?" Mark asked his friend.

"Yeah, we can do that. But we should probably do it in our blood. I mean, that's how these sorts of things work, right?" "How the fuck would I know the answer to that, Johnny?" Mark responds mockingly, as a loud crack of thunder roared through the Hallows' Eve sky. It had caught them all off-guard, making all three of them jump.

"Damn it. I thought the forecast was supposed to be clear. "Huh. Spooky. Isn't that part of what we had written? Toward the end of our story?" Johnny said, as the sky above them grumbled, like the stomach of a slumbering wild beast, that was about to awake, for its overdue and anticipated meal.

Chills came over the three boys, from the unsettling coincidence. "Ha, yeah that's actually pretty cool. But, that's for a different character" Mark said, attempting to conceal his own anxiousness. The truth was the boy was beginning to grow nervous. They all were whether they admitted it or not.

Johnny thought to himself for a moment. "Even if this crazy idea were to work. I'd feel bad for the characters. Finding out that you're not real. And what about everything else? Their entire lives would be lies. Their friends, families, their personalities. That's even worse than what we had written. Not just dead, but they're never even born. Never real to begin with. Now, that's scary" Johnny, quietly thought.

"Isn't there a word for that?" Johnny wondered. He thought back to his catechism class. "Oh, right. Anathema. That was the word" the boy thought, as he remembered the term. "A fate so horrible, it would be better to have never been born. That's what it meant."

The boy continued to think about the matter. "Not being born. Not being real? What would that feel like?" He wondered if there existed a medical term for that. It sounded too strange to be a real thing though. Such a thing would surely lead to madness.

Thunder continued to rumble, as a storm grew above the boys treehouse. "I guess it's good that we're inside here. It's convenient, at the very least. We're not going to get wet, but what if lightning hits the treehouse?" Mark inquired, peeking his head out of the treehouse window. "Well Mark, then I guess it'll really be like Frankenstein" Pete said. "Maybe that'll give it life."

"You guys are actually starting to creep me out about this silly game" Johnny said, as he began to shiver due to the drop of temperature. "Just take it easy, Johnny. Pete is just kidding around. He's only joking. This is so childish. If it weren't for us, Pete, you'd probably end up playing these games with yourself. We're a bit too old now to have imaginary friends, don't you think?"

"Well, let's hurry up. It's starting to get cold, since it's raining, now" Johnny says. "That's also like in the story, isn't it? The temperature dropping" Mark says. "I think that's kind of a stretch. It can rain on any day" Johnny replies. Mark laughs, "You think that's a stretch? But you're getting worried about everything else, as if anything could possibly happen?" Mark teased. Johnny, looked away, embarrassed and beginning to feel picked on.

"You think we should put this piece of paper inside of it? Like it's his soul?" Pete asked. "Yeah but remember to write it in our blood" Johnny said. "Why's that?" asked Mark. "I dunno, it just seems like the sort of thing we're supposed to do in a case like this" Johnny replied. "I guess I can't argue with that" said Mark.

"Alright here it goes" Pete whispered, as he pulled out a pair of scissors from his pocket. The boy sliced the tip of his index finger with the edge of the scissor's blade. The boy's blood steadily dripped down onto the paper. "Ouch!" cried Johnny, as Mark pricked the young boy's finger unexpectedly. Mark, then took the same pair of scissors, and did the same to his own flesh.

The three boys blood flowed onto the paper. Pete grabbed a nearby twig and dipped the tip of it in the puddle of blood. "What's that for?" Mark asks. "We need a writing utensil, don't we? It's not like we can just use a pen." The twig dripped with crimson droplets of blood, as Pete gingerly placed it above the piece of paper and wrote the word "Soul" on it. "There. Done" Pete said, as his two friends watched over his shoulder.

"Why are we pricking are hands with scissors? Why did you even have that with you, Pete? Oh, whatever. Let's just do this" Mark says, as Pete stuffed the paper inside of the dummy's leaf-filled shirt. Mark chuckles briefly and looked over at the clock by them.

"I can't believe you actually had a clock like that, Pete" Mark said, as they look over at the crocodile clock ticking away from the chair. "Yeah, that was oddly convenient, wasn't it?" "Ok, it's almost midnight now. I'm getting really excited", said Johnny.

Now that it was almost time. Mark felt his heart pounding in his chest. He couldn't bring himself to admit it to his friends, considering how much he had been mocking the game. Just as Mark had hid his true nervous feelings, Johnny was also becoming increasingly more concerned than he had let on. He wasn't just slightly nervous, like when Mark had teased him about it before. Although he tried to masquerade as just being excited, he was now, legitimately getting scared.

"So, our plan is to just sit here and wait till

midnight, and see if this actually works?" "Isn't that simple enough, Mark? Come one you guys, put your hands on the Ouija board. Alright, here goes nothing" Mark said. The trio of boys place their hands on the planchette residing on the board. "If we really communicate with some kind of phantom, then..." Pete says, with their hands resting just between the illustrations of the sun and moon on the board.

"I'm sorry to break this to you, but nothing's going to happen, Pete. I can't believe you convinced me to try this with you guys" muttered Mark. "Look, it's beginning to move" Johnny said, pointing with his free hand at the Ouija board.

"That's just Pete moving the piece, by himself. That's how these things work, you know? We're not even moving it at all." The three boys lean in closely and watch the board. "It's midnight now, Pete. See I told you-" Mark begins to say as he's cutoff by the sound of lightning striking the treehouse.

Chapter 18: Inferno

One of Pete's earliest memories was his father reading to him an old children's story. The Velveteen Rabbit. It was a heartwarming tale of a stuffed rabbit, who had been magically granted sentience. Throughout the story, he yearned for further awareness so he could be one with his master. Who was the young boy, who had owned the stuffed animal.

At the story's climax, the boy catches scarlet fever. All of his toys had to be burned to ensure the eradication of the disease. That included, the child's much beloved Velveteen Rabbit. The penultimate chapter had always struck Pete as a poignant one. It was a scene, which entailed the toys, burning in despair, while wishing for some kind of a miracle. The rabbit prayed, to be saved as he became consumed in a fiery blaze.

This was the memory, Pete had just thought of, as the night had taken an unexpected turn. Although in his current situation, he felt as if the roles in the story had been reversed. That the tables had been turned, and he was the burning Velveteen Rabbit in need of a miracle.

The young man lets out a cry of agony, as flames blaze through the night. It is November 1st, 12:01am. Mere moments after the game in the treehouse, Pete's body is engulfed in fire, after his treehouse had been struck by lightning. "Was it coincidence, or fate?" "Was it simply an awful turn of events, or had he brought this calamity upon himself?" Those are a couple of the questions, rushing through the boy's mind, at this very moment. Even if he were to survive this tragedy, Pete's burns may heal, yet the experience will indubitably leave an indelible mark on his soul.

"There's no way this will work" the words echo through Pete's mind as he remembers Mark's words. Dropping to his knees, Pete, writhes in agony, His burning skin rubs harshly against the wooded floor with smell of seared flesh, filling the room. "Christ, it hurts so much. I think I'm going to pass out", Pete thinks to himself, as the boy attempts to drag his flaming body to the door.

The roof of the treehouse collapses, crushing the table between. The boy senses a jolt of despair, as the burning wood now obstructed his only means of escaping the inferno. "No..." Pete weakly mutters, as he coughs out blood. It was at that moment, the boy knew this was his final Halloween.

Creaking with instability, the floor of the treehouse, shakes. The boy realized it was only a matter of time until it collapses into a fiery grave. The Ouija board, having fallen off from the crushed table, fell flat in front of the frightened child's face. "This is crazy, Pete" the voice of Mark's protests continues to ring through Pete's fading consciousness. "All that happened was that the treehouse got struck by lightning. Now, I'm going to die, from playing a stupid childish game...and it was all my idea" he tells himself.

"It's all your fault, you idiot" Mark voice scolds him. As the conflagration consumes the treehouse, Pete's vision begins to fade in and out of a waking state. The fumes of the thick black smoke fill the boys lungs. With his world blurring, and body roasting in the flames, Pete blacks out. The last thing he hears, are his friends whimpering. Too weak to let out screams anymore, their moans were like that of old dying dogs, preparing to greet the Rainbow Bridge. The mythical Valhalla for deceased pets.

Pete's eyes flutter open, as the boy finds himself in a bright room, with a nurse hovering over him. "Enough! Please be quiet. "You're just going to make your injuries worse. Just calm down and try to get some rest. You're hurt, it's going to take quite some time to heal from these burns. The hospital has contacted your mother, and she should be over here soon" the woman rattles on, trying to calm the wounded child.

With virtually no strength, Pete rolls his head to his side. It took all of his energy to simply do that, due to his weakened condition. Simply doing that, had felt like he had just bench pressed the full power of an atom bomb.

Now able to see to his side, he could discern

that he was on some sort of a stretcher, or bed. "I'm in a hospital?" the exhausted boy thinks to himself. Panicked, the nurse reaches over and administers medicine into a tube hooked into Pete's veins. "Here, this should make you calm down a bit. This will make you relax and get some sleep" she tells him, in a soothing and gentle tone. A tone, which sounded like the polar-opposite of the frantic yells and moaning in the treehouse. As the nurse, injects the solution, Pete's eyelids began slowly twitching, as if they were curtains attempting to fall down, on a closing performance.

"What was that?" Pete thought, as his perception of the world around him began to dissolve away, like a curtain being lifted on a stage revealing some type of hidden dark secret. A sense of ecstasy sets in, and heightens his curiosity "Is that...a face?" the boy wonders as he catches a glimpse behind the betwixt veil of what he understands as reality and what awaits in the great beyond.

Pete's eyelids were now fluttering as irregularly as the erratic palpitations of his heart. His thoughts, now every bit as tempestuous as the storm which brought disaster upon the night. Like the lightning bolt struck the treehouse, or a gale ripping through a maelstrom, Pete felt his heart begin to pound. "Doctor come quick" shouts the nurse as she sees the boy's vital signs drastically plummet.

The monitor on the machine hooked up to Pete's vitals, flickers and flashes a red light. It lets out a beeping alarm, as the nurse eyeballs the device in confusion. It was clear the boy's health was in serious jeopardy, and she did not know what to do. Tears form at the corner of her eyes, as she turns to a man in a white jacket, running toward her.

Like an urgent understudy in a stage play gone terribly awry, a doctor swiftly enters the room. "He's going into shock" a garbled voice mutters. In his now delirious state, Pete was unable to discern who the voice had come from. Both the doctor's and nurse's voices, had become nearly inaudible to the young man. In his dazed state, Pete glanced upward at the aghast medical practitioners. As the understaffed emergency room, hectically struggled to prevent the cataclysmic night from descending into a full-scale catastrophe, the boy moans in disoriented misery.

"Stay with me, kid" Pete hears a voice spout out in desperation. The voice was barely audible to the child, but he managed to make out that much, before he lost his focus, and it became incoherent to him. The boys vision increases to blur as madness begins to consume him. "Mark? Johnny? They need help, too. Mark had called out to them before, why are they not helping them? Did they even survive? Mark was right" Pete thinks to himself. "This is all my fault. They should be helping my friends first, instead of me."

Darkness. Pete's vision cuts to black. This phenomenon happens, when the body is overwhelmed, to conserve it's resources. Like when someone passes out from a high fever, or in extreme instances, such as Pete's.

Although his vision was failing him, Pete's other senses, remained, albeit distorted. A foul stench fills his nostrils, and Pete felt droplets of a wet substance fall upon his arm. Pete shakes from the cold fluid and attempts to brush it off. The boy's arm is held back firmly, and it dawns on him that what he felt, must've been fluid dripping on him from a syringe.

Pete's suspicions are confirmed, when the boy felt what he assumes must be a needle piercing his burnt flesh. It stabbed deep into his skin as if a fine piece of cutlery slicing into an overdone slab of steak. "What is that? Is that more morphine? Or maybe, it's fentanyl" Pete thought, as he remembered back to one of his science classes at school. "I hope it is. That should get rid of my pain. There's a reason people get addicted to that kind of stuff. It's supposed to feel really good" the boy thinks, as delirium takes hold of his mind.

There were many things racing through Pete's mind right now. But most of all, even more than whether or not he would live, was the vague visage which he caught a glimpse of just before completely losing awareness. No, not the faces of the nurse, doctor or any other medical staff in the emergency room, a different one. Although it had only happened for less than a second, Pete thought he caught a glimpse of another face.

"Who was it?" he wondered, as his mind entered an unfamiliar plane of consciousness. Pete, thought that the face he had seen, looked so surprised to see him. Whoever or whatever that thing was- it seemed like it was hiding. As if it were like a child playing hide and seek. Was it hiding from him? Had he found it? Or was it looking for him all along?

As Pete's mind continues to phase into oblivion, he hears a tumultuous chattering noise, rise from out of the abyss. The boy's green eyes fill with blood, as his lids close. His closing lids, now as if a crimson curtain, slowly falling down as the noises fade away into the night. Thinking he's about to face death, the boy reflects. "These noises remind me even more of the writing we did. About Peter Pan. How clapping can bring back the dead, as long as you have an imagination."

Chapter 19: Purgatorio

"This can't be real" Pete thinks as he frantically turns side to side. He was now standing in an all too familiar location. Or rather, several locations, simultaneously. The realm he found himself in, was like a blurred hodgepodge of what he thought only existed in his imagination.

He was somehow within the places from the story he had written. Looking to his left, Pete saw the front door of the household his fictitious family had resided in. The door opens, and a familiar phantasm stepped out, from out of it. It was Joe, from his writings. "Here you go" he chimes, as he holds up a jar of candy toward him.

Looking to his right, stood a mirror. A bathroom mirror, specifically. Gingerly, Pete approached it and gazed deeply into the glistening glass. Before his eyes, a reflection which was not his own, began to materialize. Although it was a face he had never seen before, he recognized it in an instant, due to the detailed writing he had done. It was Rafe, the eldest brother from his story. Appearing just as surprised as Pete was, Rafe's visage forms a terrified look of recognition. The face screams, and in an instant, the glass shatters into pieces.

Pete attempts to shield his face from the breaking glass but cannot find the strength to lift his arms. His concern about the glass, is moot as he shifts his view downward, and discovers an even worse predicament. The young man feels his body shake and possessing an appearance which was not his own. Mustering what little strength he had, caused his arms to shake, weakly. "What's this?" Pete thinks, as his eyeballs roll to the corner of his vision. Auburn colored leaves slowly spill out of what should be his torso, and two twigs from a tree, bulge out where his arms should be.

His body had been morphed into that of the CPR-dummy, from earlier. Pete looks forward, and grimly realizes the occurrence. Transported again, he was now in front of the table from his treehouse, Pete can see the Ouija board resting on it. "Hello, Pete" read a note atop the board. "Is it really him?" A disembodied voice whispers omni-presently within the room. "Jimmy" Pete thinks. The voice he had heard, was just how he had imagined his character Jimmy would sound, if ever heard him.

In front of the board, materialized the amusement park stage from his writing, as did several ghostly figures. A clanging noise catches Pete's attention, and he rolls his eyes to look upward. Above him stood a grand chandelier, and the boy heard what sounded like the clipping of scissors. Swaying side to side, the chandelier falls and crashes downward. Unable to flee, Pete clenched his eyes shut, and in a flash, hears a roar of thunder.

Pete is then communicated a message, in what can only be described as by means of pure thoughtform. A message, which was delivered by means described by some with clairvoyance as telepathy. It was brief, but nonetheless concise in its message. "We're happy to see you again, even if it's only for this one time. We love you, Pete."

"Is that what you expected us to say? That we love you? You? A false god who wrote us into a fake existence of suffering?" The message continued, now in normal audible human language. The light on the stage, begins to illuminate. Standing on the stage, the bright light shines onto the figures upon it. On the stage, were Pete's creations; Joe, Rafe and Jimmy.

When Pete had written them, he based the characters on his friends. Rafe, reflected Mark's more pessimistic nature, while Jimmy has had a warmer more friendly attitude, as did his friend Johnny. Initially, he was worried that Jimmy sounded too similar to Johnny, but decided to leave it in, thinking maybe he could leave it as a sort of clue. To see if his friends, would notice that during their brainstorming, he had based the archetypes the characters possessed, on them.

Although, it wouldn't have been too far-fetched. They knew Pete was already a pretty good reader and writer as it was. Certainly, at the top of his class in that regard. So, it wouldn't have been inconceivable that he would use a writing technique such as that.

This fact was probably why he was able to lead them in writing a story, with a richer vocabulary than usual for kids his age. But now, these characters he had written about were not the same. That was beginning to grow increasingly evident to Pete, as the events continued to unfold.

"Yes, we all know what's going on. We always have. You think we're nothing more than the characters you wrote us as? What we went through, was like what reading off a script is like for actors. Nothing more than a charade we went through to get here" their message continues, as the three figures step off of the stage toward Pete.

"Despite the facade we've all lived, the emotions we felt were very real to us. Some of them, at least. The horror was. The horror, of knowing you're not real. That's why we were feeling that sense of unreality all along, wasn't it? Discovering the reality that you don't exist. It's an anxiety so extreme, the medical world had to create a word to describe it.

"Derealization-Depersonalization. Probably the same term used in scriptures, to describe Hell. Anathema. A fate so terrible, it would be better to have never been born. That's quite a statement, isn't it? Could you imagine what you would do if you felt such a thing? Can you imagine what you would do if you found the one responsible for it? What you would do to them?" the voice said, coldly.

"We're going to show you exactly that. You wanted to find us, well now you have. The game of hide and seek, is over. Now it's time for your prize" they said all speaking in unison. Jimmy's hand clenches a pair of scissors, and he raises it toward Pete's face. The boy opens the pair of scissors, sticking the two blades into each of Pete's nostrils.

Pete groans, as he feels the sharp pain of the blades. The physical sensation made Pete realize that he was now in a normal physical form, once again. However, considering the circumstances, that was not exactly favorable.

The three figures laugh, as blood trickles from out of Pete's nose. Lightly twisting the scissors, Jimmy pulls the scissors out and hold's it to Pete's throat. "How about we stick him in the oven? Let's roast him" Joe says. "Good idea, Dad. We can have him for dinner. " Rafe, adds.

Overpowered by his three creations, Pete squirms in a futile attempt to escape their clutches. "Stay still, you're not going anywhere, little brother" Rafe taunts, as they proceed to drag Pete over toward the kitchen oven from his story, as the location transforms, again. The kitchen oven begins to form in his midst, as a cloud of black smoke flows through the cracks of its door. With an ear piercing clang, the oven door opens. Like a vacuum set in reverse, the inside of the oven sucks Pete toward it, with colossal force. Pete is thrusted inside the maw of the oven, as it's door slams shut, like the jaws of a primal beast. Once more, the boy is overcome with darkness, as Pete's transported to the deep abyss.

"Where is this place?" Pete thinks to himself. He was unable to move, or sense his body, whatsoever. Not understanding how or why, the boy steadily began to notice that his thoughts seemed to project his existence. He is without form, in a realm one can only describe as like looking through a kaleidoscope. Strange fractal shapes pop in and out of existence, all around him.

The boy's vision was now like that of a dragonfly's. Perception, in all 360 degrees around him. He's no longer limited by his former senses. Touch, sight, smell, yes, he still had all of those senses, despite his disembodied, nonphysical form. In addition to, he now had countless other senses, which existed beyond Pete's limited human grasp.

We've all heard of the expression of something being like "trying to explain color to a blind man." This occurrence was deeper than that. It was more akin to imagining what it was like to have antennas or attempting to explain a complex mathematical equation to your pet. Now, amplify that ineffable sensation, a thousand times, and you'll begin to understand the idea.

Vibrant colors, flew like a wild tempest, giving his mind a sensory overload. The mysterious realm felt eerily familiar to the boy. Pete, wondered if perhaps this realm, is where he came from. Where everyone came from, before they're were born.

"Welcome" a voice greets Pete. It communicates with him through some other means of communication he's not familiar with. Not through a voice box, or through pictures, or words. But with one of the new senses, that had only just been revealed to him. "Long time no see" the voice, says to the boy. Pete cannot tell if it is the same being, or a different one talking to him now. Putting labels on these creatures, seemed meaningless. So, did numbering them as individuals, or a collective. He could not grasp how, but they appeared to transcend our understanding of what being was.

One of these entities, materializes in front of Pete, as if he were a member of an audience, and privileged enough to receive a front row seat. Looking at it, with all of his frightening new senses, made the boy feel overwhelmed. The sensation felt to him like his mind were a computer about to overheat. Not at all dissimilar to that of a dog's mind, which suddenly had the consciousness of a human's mind uploaded into it.

"I can't take this. It's too much" Pete cries out to the being. The entity emits an emotion he never felt before. As a man would erupt with laughter from hearing a great joke they haven't heard before, or cry in anguish, or despair, after a horrific accident. The release of the display of emotion, was perhaps one man wasn't meant to understand.

Astounded, Pete tries to make sense of the being. It appeared to always be in motion, like some sort of machine. He felt as if he were an insect, coming across a human being for the first time, and tried hopelessly to make sense out of the matter.

It's playful way of moving, reminded Pete of cartoon characters. Like that of jesters or elves. All moving together in unison, like some sort of grand engine. Pete wondered if these are where the archetypes for all different sorts of mythological creatures came from. Imps, genies, leprechauns. Perhaps, even angels and demons. "Was this their origin?" he asked himself. Different cultures over time, describing the same thing. Maybe, where most people got the idea of alien abductions from, too. His manner of understanding had felt elevated. Not just from that of a child's to an adult's, but to something even beyond.

Pete doesn't feel threatened, by the creatures. However, he knew he was in way over his head. Like he had stumbled upon a secret room that he was not supposed to have entered. A place, unknown to man, and familiar only to eternity.

It dawns on the boy, that he can no longer remember his name. "Am I having amnesia?" Pete asks the creatures. They release a strange outburst of the unfamiliar emotion, yet again. They manage to communicate to him through one of his new senses, that his question was silly. That his old identity, is of no use here. That in this strange realm, no one has names, anymore. That they're all part of the same thing, and that we all always have been.

Their response upsets the boy, and he released a strange burst of emotions, himself. This seems to amuse them, as he's not as developed as they are. "They're mocking me" Pete thought. Expressing themselves non-semantically, the beings continue their mind boggling expressions. They begin to swirl together into what can only be described as like a spiraling jigsaw-puzzle. Each one of them, forming a piece of a greater whole.

Once the beings unite together, they stood over the boy, as an awe-inspiring and terrible figure. Pete trembled in terror and confusion. The overwhelming transference of information was already too great for the boy to handle, but it continued to grow further. They were trying to communicate some kind of complex idea to him. As if, showing him the blueprints to the reality he had known to be his own. Two red holes opened up at the top of the being and peered down at him.

"Are those its eyes?" Pete asked himself. It seemed the being, was trying to form an anthropomorphic visage, to better suit the young man's intellectual limitations. Another gap, which opened wide, appeared below its eyes. It had now formed a mouth. It opened, and a pointed appendage forming a tongue slithered out of it. It's tongue, rattles with the vibrato of a great opera singer, as horns, sprouted atop it's head. It's torso, spiraled down to infinity, as if the tail of a never ending serpent.

Pete's world, began to dissolve away, and his vision became fuzzy. Almost like a television set losing its reception. Everything goes black. What feels like an eternity, passes. As the room fades, Pete begins to feel himself fall into a trance like state. The sensation was as if slipping into a warm bath. A sedated, and helpless state. The boy didn't exactly feel any pain, but he was cognizant enough to realize that he was being put into another vulnerable situation. Like the Sirens, who attempted to lure Odysseus to his death, Pete feared he was about to become prey to a cunning predator.

Additional creatures appear at the boys side. Beasts, which carved their way into this strange reality, tearing through it at a breakneck pace, with minimal effort. Instantly, Pete recognized these phantoms from childhood night terrors he had thought he had long forgotten.

The boy felt a cold sensation, as if he were now cold blooded. This sudden realization made Pete cognizant that he had form, yet again. Furthermore, he was now at another place he thought was nothing more than pure fiction. Looking downward at his hands, the young man discovers he is in yet another foreign body. No, not the CPR Dummy, or a body of any human form for that matter. The vessel he was in now, held little semblance to human anatomy. Scaly appendages appear in place of his arms, hands legs, and feet. "My teeth? I seem to have so many" he thought to himself, as a shred of his memory returns.

"I feel so hungry" Pete thinks to himself, as his newly formed stomach growls. Now in the illusion of a corporal plane, the boy looks over in the direction of other beings. Innocent laughter. Next to him, Pete could hear the sounds of children at play. Nature takes control over him, as he begins to approach the laughing children. A loud thump catches Pete's attention and he turns to its point of origin. It was himself. It was him, as he had written himself in the story. An identical copy of himself, trips and falls down, beside him. Lying on his side, his double stares at him. Tiny green eyes stare back into his wide green ones, as Pete's jaw opens and mouth salivates.

Pete's double screams in terror, as Pete's primal urges completely take over. He was now no longer possessing any sense of right or wrong, only an insatiable appetite. A symphony of screams rings loudly, amongst the chaos, as Pete feasts upon his own flesh. It's not till he's finished that common sense returns to Pete's mind. Tears begin to form, and for the first time ever, a crocodile cries for real. Realizing what he had done, Pete gazes upward, overcome with a jolt of anxiety induced delirium. In his inebriated state of mind, Pete could see a mysterious, yet familiar figure above him.

"What is that? Some kind of book?" Pete frantically thought to himself, as he notices that the figure hovering above him, was indeed grasping something in its hands. Pete begins to wonder what the object could be. It's eyes, peer down at Pete like, two scorching hot suns on a desert day, as he realizes who it is.

Another wave of hunger overcomes the boy, as Pete turns his attention to his victim, and begins to feast once more. With his teeth ripping through the flesh and sinew of his dinner, Pete becomes distracted by the presence hovering above him, again. The familiar figure was grasping an item in its hands, which Pete couldn't help but become increasingly fixated on. Once more, Pete glances upward at it, turning his attention toward its presence.

Forgotten memories flow back to him, as Pete's sanity reaches its breaking point. The essence of his very being screams at its core. Pete's body and soul are both torn asunder. He was now, as if fluid in a blender. Both intact, and one in the same. His

181

consciousness also remains within it. Inseparable. His body, along with his consciousness, had all become embedded into one. As if Pete's every being, were condensed into a sort of binding. Like a tightly binded leather bound novel. A book, which contained the pages of his life. Cover to cover, clamped shut by the jaws of eternity.

It was as if it were a crocodile-skin, leather bounded novel. This was the book, the mysterious figure was reading. It was his life. His soul bounded within the pages of the book, and that he only ever existed within the mind of the being reading it. The image of the book became increasingly more evident, as Pete gazed upon it. It had a black background, and a depiction of a crocodile on it's cover.

Looking at the figure, the truth of its mysterious identity had indeed dawned upon Pete. It was the character that he and his friends had written about. The one he named after his pet snake. No, it was not Jimmy, Rafe or Joe. He had already met all the rest of the characters in the book, but it was this one, the one who was reading about them that was now at last showing its face. At least, with what little of its face Pete could make out.

Pete thought that if he and his friends kept this character removed from most of the direct events, they could minimize any potential dangers. That is, if their experiment worked out in the end. However, this was not the eventuality he anticipated.

Thunder booms, as the entire vicinity of the realm, trembles. In a flash, the old life Pete knew came storming back to him. Like a calm tide gently drifting back to shore, after a wild storm.

The transition starts off hazily at first, but then it comes rushing back. "You okay, Pete?" Johnny asks, turning to Pete's side. "What? Y-Yeah, I'm fine" Pete responds. Thinking to himself, Pete reflects on the madness. "My mind is foggy. The past few moments, feel like some kind of dazed blur" Pete contemplates. It had felt to him, like the waking moments, after a dream.

Slowly, the former hysteria fades from Pete's mind. He and his friends were all once more, among each other in their treehouse. "Hey Pete, what's wrong?" Mark asks, as he and Johnny look at him with inquisitive expressions. Pete blinks in bewilderment. "Oh...I-It's nothing, you guys." he tells them.

"I'm back in the treehouse? Did I ever really leave?" Pete thinks to himself. Contemplating his existence, Pete looks at his friends, and at the Ouija board on the table.

"Pete, your nose" Johnny says pointing at him. "What do you-" Pete lifts his hand to his nose, and rubs it. Looking at his hand, Pete sees a bit of blood on it. "Just a nosebleed. Don't worry about it" Pete says, as he forms a smile.

Chapter 20: Paradiso

"See? Nothing happened, Pete" Mark says pointing to the crocodile clock in the treehouse, indicating that it was past midnight. "Yeah. Well, it was still worth a shot" Johnny says, with a chuckle. A flash of light, gleams from out of their window, as booming noise, rings through the boys eardrums.

"Woah, that was really close. The treehouse could have been struck by that bolt" Johnny remarks, as the three boys look at one another. "W-What the hell?" Mark says, jumping out of his chair. Mark points to the Ouija board, and both Johnny and Pete turn their attention toward it.

At the center of the board, a spark of light flickered, and a flame slowly began spreading over it. Acting quickly, Pete grabs the bottle of holy water he had on the table, and speedily extinguishes the flame. "I guess it's a good thing you brought that bottle, after all" Johnny said.

"How did that happen?" Did ash or something fly in through the window from the lightning bolt?" Mark asks, trying to make sense out of the occurrence. "That's just too weird" Johnny says, in exasperation.

"Come on you guys, let's go. It's pouring out, anyway" Pete responds. "Yeah, we don't want the treehouse to get struck, next" Johnny said, peeking out of the window, as light sparkled in the clouds above. Mark and Johnny, begin to gather their belongings, when Pete pauses, momentarily. A pensive look comes across the boy's face, when Johnny notices it. "What is it, Pete?" Johnny inquires, wondering why his friend had such a solemn expression.

"You ever have the feeling where you know you forgot something? I just had that feeling right now, for some reason" Pete tells him. It's true, Pete had no recollection of the bewildering experience, he had just endured. It had slowly faded away. In its place, he was left with a strange sense of uneasiness.

Exiting the treehouse, Pete climbs down it's ladder and approaches his home. A woman's voice echoes from the distance. "Alright Pete, come inside now and change out of your costume!" Hearing the woman's voice, Pete rushes toward her.

"Oh my" remarks Pete's mother, April. Johnny and Mark approach the foot of Pete's front door, dressed as the Phantom of the Opera and Sherlock Holmes. "Well, it was good seeing you guys. Nice costume, Pete" Mark chuckles as he walks off. "Yeah, see you later." Johnny says, as he joins Mark, parting for their homes. As his friends walk away, Pete looks over at his mother.

"Who's trick or treating costume do you think was the best?" Pete inquires, pointing to the costume he still had on. "They're all great. Now change out of your costume. No more playing make believe.

Halloween is over, and it's time to get ready for bed"
the woman stated realizing the night had concluded,

"What's that, Pete?" April asks him as the two
approach the front door of the house. There seemed
to be shadows of sort, at their doorstep. "Is that from
the storm clouds?" April asks, as she and her son
look up toward the Halloween's night sky.
Pete and his mother, gaze at the black abyss above
them. Numerous stars reside over their heads.
Twinkling in the sky, they peered down at them, as if
eyes looking down at pets in an aquarium. Looking
at the night's sky above, made Pete think about the
vivarium he keeps his pet snake in. About how when
he looked inside it, he often contemplated what was
going on inside of the creature's reptilian brain.

A sensation of being watched comes over the
two of them. As if they themselves, were also just
caged creatures. That their cage, was the Earth they
knew. Clouds pass above them, as if hands turning
the pages of their lives. The passing clouds felt like
a hand waving hello. Or perhaps rather, the hands of
someone waving goodbye.

April looked at Pete, as he walked up the stairs
holding a mask in his hand. Pete, glances back at her
with his green eyes. "Goodnight, Mom" the boy
says to her. "Goodnight, Pete. I don't know about
you, but I'm glad this Halloween has finally come to
an end."

At last, in his bedroom, Pete, looked over at the

vivarium standing near his nightstand. It sat alongside a jar of candy corn. Slowly, Pete walks over to the caged creature inside, and glances down at it. Looking at his pet snake inside, Pete smiles and breathes a sigh of relief. "How are you doing? Did you have a fun Halloween, too?" he says out loud, talking to his pet snake.

Opening the top of the cage, Pete extends his hand into it. Gently, Pete rubs his fingers down the serpent, petting it in a soothing fashion. Sitting down on his bed, the young man opens up his notebook, and turns to the last page. Holding up a crayon he begins drawing on it. "I'm not much of an artist, but what do you think?" the boy says as he lifts the opened notebook toward the vivarium, proudly showing his drawing to the snake inside.

"I think it looks just like you. I'm almost done drawing it" Pete remarks. "I wonder what made me want to draw this, all of a sudden" Pete wonders, putting the drawing down. His drawing was that of a snake eating its tail. At last retiring for some much needed sleep, Pete turns off the light, and rests his head on the pillow. Opening his green eyes once more, he turns to his side in the direction of his pet snake. "Goodnight. Happy Halloween."

Chapter 21: Winter

The vibrant colors of the fallen autumn leaves die out as the days pass by. Autumn turns to winter, as pure white snow, deprived of all color takes the leaves place in the subsequent season. In his home, Pete sits with his mother April, as he sits on the couch reading in their living room. The young man leisurely reads a horror novel, while his mother watches the news on their television set. "Hey Mom? Could you turn up that up, please?" the boy asks. Being across the living room, the program had caught the child's attention. Reaching for the remote, April obliges, and adjusts the volume.

"Sure, honey" April says smiling, as the raising sound of the news anchor on the set, gradually increases. Looking at the television screen, Pete watches a man in a vibrant Hawaiian shirt, begin a news report. "Welcome back! This is Sam, reporting with the best news in town. Thanks for tuning in. The much anticipated construction of Nightmare Land has finally reached it's end and will be open to the general public just in time for Christmas. The owner of the castle himself, will be offering a sneak peek to its first eager customers, starting tomorrow on Christmas Eve" the man on the television set, shouts. According to the spokespeople, the mysterious project wants their grand opening to represent a Christmas gift to the community. Now, for the weather..." the man concludes, as the program continues its report.

"Nightmare Land? What's that?" Pete asks his mother, shifting his attention from his book to the television broadcast. "You mean you haven't heard?" she says, in a baffled, yet amused tone. Pete shakes his head. "No? Should I have?" the boy asks, embarrassed. His mother's stunned response had made him feel like an outsider hearing an inside joke, he had been obliviously left out of.

"I guess most boys your age don't really watch the news, very often. Since you're still so young. Not to mention, you're always so busy with your schoolwork. Anyway, it's about that big building they've been building close to downtown. Surely, you must've at least seen some pictures of it. The advertisements have been all over the place" she tells him, as the journalist on the television walks in front of what looks like a towering castle.

"Look, that's it" April says, pointing at the television screen. "Just the other day, some old lady on my commute, was trying to talk to me about the place. She was handing out pamphlets, promoting the place. Normally, I wouldn't mind at all. I took one of her flyers, but she was being too pushy about it. Insisting, that I just had to go to the building" the woman tells her son.

"Her intentions seemed well enough, though. She was saying they're holding some sort of dinner for the homeless people in the city around when the place opens up. There are a lot of homeless people in the city, so it's nice to see a company with benevolent goals in mind, like that" April says.

"You referred to the place as a building. But, it's so big, it looks more like a castle, to me, Mom" Pete replies. "Very observant, Pete. That's because it is. Or at least was, historically speaking, that is" his mother answers, smiling at him, while stirring a cup of tea in her hand. "It looks kind of scary" Pete says, as the man on TV continues his report.

"Well, it should be. That's not just any castle. It's one that was recently brought from Europe and reconstructed here. It's called Bran Castle. Or at least it was till it's relocation." Pete's head tilt's, as he awaits his mother's explanation. "I don't think I follow. Bran Castle? What's that?" the boy asked, unaware of the significance, of the name, and of its history.

"That's the name of Count Dracula's castle" his mother tells him. "Wow, that's cool" the boy responds. "You know, your father used to live around that area when he was a boy, right? He immigrated here long ago, from Transylvania. It's a shame he never got a chance to go back there to visit, before he died. I've never been to Romania, so it would have been a nice vacation idea. But, in a strange way, I guess it's like part of your father is returning home to us, right? Now that they've reconstructed that castle here, maybe it'll give us an idea about what it was like for your dad growing up in that part of the world. Your father said he didn't want to go back there though. It's a shame" April said, as she lifted her teacup to her face.

"He didn't? Why not?" Pete asked her. "Your father was a wonderful man, but he had some superstitions. You know how it is, where people grow up hearing scary stories about their homeland. Cultural stuff like that. It's especially the case, when they come from there, themselves" April said, sipping her tea.

"Ha, you mean Dad actually believed in vampires?" Pete asks her, snickering as he found the notion silly. April, begins to chuckle herself, causing a bit of the tea of spurt out of her nose. "You shouldn't make people laugh like that when they're in the middle of drinking something, Pete" she says with a laugh.

"Sorry, Mom" Pete says, amused. Reaching for a napkin to wipe her nose, April sets her teacup down. "No. You misunderstand. That's not what I meant. I guess I should be a little more specific by what I meant. He didn't believe in vampires. But he was still nonetheless, superstitious. Making sure not to walk under ladders, or step on cracks. Those sorts of things" she tells her son.

"Well, if it's not vampires, then what do you mean?" Pete asks, confused. "Odd as it seems, when you talk about the actual real life Dracula to many people from the area, it doesn't have exactly the same connotations it does here in the US. Most of them don't think vampires really exist. I'm sure some crazy people out there do, but your father certainly did not. But many people from the area do think there was something supernatural about the man. About the real life version of Dracula" she explains.

"This is so weird, Mom. Look at the book I was just reading. Here, check it out" Pete says, as he lifts a softcover novel from the couch. "What's that?" she says, standing up out of her chair, toward the boy. Walking closer, the woman approaches the couch Pete's was reading it on. Now across from her son, April extends her arm as Pete hands her his book.

April inspects the book. "Bram Stoker's Dracula" his mother says out loud, reading the book's title from the cover. "That is kind of spooky, Pete. Don't worry, I'm sure it's just a coincidence" she says brushing his hair quickly, in a playful manner.

"Stop that! You'll mess up my hair" Pete exclaims. "I'm just joking around, Pete" she says to the boy. "It's alright, I know" Pete tells her, as she puts her arm back down to her side.

Did you know that Count Dracula was based on a real person? I don't know much about him. I know a little, only because of what your father told me, back when he was alive. So, in a way that horror novel is based on some truth. As opposed to The Phantom of the Opera, for instance" she said to her son.

"Huh, it's funny you should say it like that" Pete says, thinking about all the references to the story about The Phantom of the Opera he and his friends, had written in their project during October. "So, what was it that Dad and other people thought was supernatural about him?" Pete asks, as his mother hands the boy back his novel.

"Vlad Dracula. That was his name. He was otherwise known as Vlad the Impaler, from people he had executed and strung out in a forest near his castle. That's what he was known as. I think I read somewhere that his surname means Dragon, or some kind of a serpent. I'm not a historian or anything, or even remotely knowledgeable about Romanian culture. But, it's pretty well documented that he was a pretty evil man, so that lead to all sorts of tales and legends about him" April explained to her curious son.

Stretching out her arms, now that she was standing up, April let's out a fatigued yawn, and continues her explanation to the boy. "Anyway, there are all sorts of various stories about him. Most of them, make believe. Due to the infamy of his life. Most of the stories, had gotten totally blown out of proportion, and that lead to all the vampire movies, and books like the one you were reading. To a lot of the people who grew up around his castle, the man was no laughing matter. Even generations after he had died, people were afraid to go into his castle. Whether he was a vampire, or just a person like you and me" April says, walking toward the kitchen.

"I never knew Dad was such a superstitious man, Mom" Pete says, as he follows his mother, exiting the living room. "Don't worry, it's not just him. Like I said, it's a cultural thing with many people who either lived there or immigrated from that area" April says as she walked into the kitchen and up to the refrigerator in the room.

"A lot of the people there think he was so evil, that he could have actually been the devil, himself. Or at least some kind of demon" she said, reaching her hand inside of the freezer. What are you looking for in there, Mom?" Pete asks, as he can see that his mother was struggling to find something in particular in the freezer.

"Just tonight's dinner. Give me a second" she answers, pulling out a large box, covered in ice, just like the snowy sidewalks outside of their house. Cold icy mist, emits from the opened freezer, giving Pete goosebumps. "Mom, close that. You're making it cold in here" he tells her. "Sorry, Pete" she says, slamming the freezer door shut.

"So, why did they bring the castle here, and change the name? Didn't people already travel to Europe to go see it?" Pete inquires. "It's probably a marketing scheme. To attract tourism, and potential customers" she says, brushing the ice off the box.

"We should go, now that the place is opening up, sometime" she says to her son. "Yeah, I guess we could go see it. "That is, if it's not too expensive" April says. "You mean they charge people just to come look at it?" Pete asks, clearly thinking that it sounded like a shrewd and unfair business strategy.

"Oh, right. You're just finding out about this place, so I guess you wouldn't know" she says as the woman places the box on the kitchen counter. "Know? Know what?" Pete asks her. "They didn't just bring that big castle here for the heck of it. God knows how many millions it must've cost to buy it from whoever the former owner was" she says, as she opens a drawer in the kitchen.

"They've turned it into a massive hotel. Not just that, but a really big theme park, too. You know? Like Disneyland, or Universal Studios. It sounds really neat to me, don't you think, Pete?" April says to her son. "It's like it can be Halloween all year, having a spooky castle here, like that" she says to the boy.

"Uh. Yeah" Pete says, as he remembers the writing he had done. "What the hell? It's different, but the idea sort of sounds like the one my friends and I had in our story" Pete thought to himself. "I bet people back in Transylvania, are actually glad they managed to sell and relocate the castle. Sure, it brought tourism to that town and country, but I have a feeling they're glad to be finally rid of it. Due to all the people who are still superstitious and fearful about it" April says, as she now begins to shuffle through the drawer, looking for something.

Pete sighs. His mother was becoming distracted from the conversation by whatever it was she was searching for. "What are you looking for now, Mom?" Pete asks her. "Scissors, to open this damn box. So, we can fucking eat, already!" she says violently moving her hand inside the drawer.

Startled by his mother's sudden loss of composure, Pete flinches. "Ah-ha! Here it is" she exclaims, pulling a pair of scissors out of the drawer. "Oh, sorry sweetheart. I shouldn't get angry and swear like that, in front of you" she says apologetically. "M-Mom, your hand" Pete says, as he points at her hand clutching the scissors.

"O-Oh. I must've accidently cut myself when my hand was in there. I guess I was moving my hand about pretty erratically, when I lost my temper, there" she observed, holding her hand up in front of her. "I guess so. Are you okay? Should I go look for a bandage, or anything?" Pete asks, looking at his mother's bleeding hand. "I can go find some hydrogen peroxide to clean your cut with, if you want. I think there's some in the bathroom" Pete says, motioning toward the direction of where he thought the item to be.

"No, don't worry about it. It's nothing, though. The cut's not that deep" she says, turning on the sink. The woman places her hand under the running water and begins to clean the wound. April holds a wash-cloth over her cut, and grabs the scissors, again. She begins cutting the box open and tears off it's lid.

"So, what's for dinner, Mom?" Pete asked, hoping that his mother had calmed down. "Take a look" April says, brushing off the remaining ice from the box. Pete's eyes nearly bulge out of their sockets, when he sees the illustration on the cover.

It was a picture of an alligator. No, not a real alligator. But a very cartoonish depiction of a man wearing an alligator mask as the product's logo. "I don't think either of us, have ever had anything this exotic for dinner before" April proclaims, with a wide smile.

"No. I don't think I ever have" Pete said, in disbelief as he thought back again, to his story. It was slightly different, being that it was an alligator, and not a crocodile. But Pete knew that crocodiles were not legal to purchase for food, anyway.

"What? Did you think I was just going to make duck again?" April says laughing. I think it's going to be great. Look how much there is" she says, commenting on the size of the box. "I don't think I've ever cooked anything in the oven this big" the woman remarked, as she turned on a switch on the oven, beginning the meal's preparations.

"Don't worry. If there's too much food, that just means we'll have lots of leftovers for ourselves, tomorrow. Oh, speaking of which, let's try to go to the grand opening that they're talking about on TV. I read on the brochure I got the other day, that there's a discount for families, when it opens tomorrow" she says in excitement.

"M-Mom. You don't think there could be like...some kind of a curse with that castle, then?" Pete asks her, with a stutter. "Aww, don't worry sweety" she says placing her cut hand on the side of the boy's face. A smudge of blood trickles off of her hand, and down Pete's cheek. His mother smiles, looking into his green eyes. "Everything's going to be just fine" she tells him.

"I know what you're probably thinking. That amusement park, resort or whatever you want to call it. Is it damned or something because of the pieces they used when that bought that old castle? No. It might make for an interesting horror movie, but they're nothing more than chunks of marble and stone. That kind of thing only happens in scary stories. Not in real life" she reassures her son.

"Now go get ready for dinner. I have a feeling, we're going to have a fun day, tomorrow" April instructs. "Okay, Mom" Pete responds, now feeling more than slightly unnerved. "What was going on?" Pete thought to himself, as he halts, abruptly.

"On second thought...I'm feeling really tired, Mom. Is it okay if I just go to bed early?" the boy asks, desperate to avoid eating the meal. Normally, he was an adventurous eater. Pete didn't mind trying different types of cuisine to eat. However, this was more than a little different. Given the situation, the idea grossed him out. "Oh, are you sure, Pete? What about your supper?" April asks her son. "Well, I'm really not that hungry" Pete says, having completely lost his appetite. There was just no way he could eat that meal considering the circumstances.

"That's fine. Goodnight, Petey" April says as she kisses her son on the cheek. Pete goes up to his room, and awaits the next day, with the greatest sense of unease he had felt since Halloween night. "I don't know what's going on, but I have a bad feeling about this" Pete thinks to himself, as he wonders if he somehow brought this all on himself. Like a deal with a money's paw, it's just as the old saying goes; Be careful what you wish for. It just might come true.

Chapter 22: The Woman in Black

Light shines down from out of Pete's bedroom window, beaming directly at the sleeping boy's face. It was the morning sun, shining down upon him, heavily. Like when the day's light shines down upon a vampire's coffin, the garish illumination awoke the slumbering young man.

Rubbing his eyes in discomfort, Pete crawled out of his bed and closed his curtains. Now closed, the thick curtains shielded the boy's eyes from the daylight. "I barely had any sleep at all last night. How could I?" Pete thinks to himself, as the day was now beginning to come to fruition.

"Almost time, Pete. Get ready" the boy's mother's voice boom from downstairs. Due to the paper thin walls of their house, Pete could hear her bellowing as if she were right there with him, in his room. "Okay, Mom" he calls back to her. "I can't believe we're about to do this" Pete thinks, nervously.

Pete was on his winter break, so he had a lot of spare time now, since he didn't have to worry about his homework. He didn't necessarily dislike going to school, but at this moment he realized just how much he'd rather be in class. "I never thought I'd be doing something like this. Especially not on Christmas Eve" the boy thought to himself, as he prepared to go downstairs.

"Are we going straight there, Mom? We still have some time to kill, don't we?" Pete inquires, hoping he can use the spare time to get out of his obligation of eating the leftover dinner, from the other night. "Now that you mention it, I suppose we do. How about the market they have set up, downtown? We'll still need to go to the parking garage they have for the castle, but that's relatively close by" April inquires. "A castle with a parking garage?" The notion sounded unusual to the boy. Then again, so did the whole idea of a theme park, also being a resort.

"Yeah, okay. That's fine" Pete said, relieved his idea worked. "Alright then, it's decided. In that case, don't spoil your appetite. We'll head right over there, whenever you're ready. "Sounds good, Mom" Pete says, as the boy and his mother, prepare to head out into the chilly winter day.

The two of them get into April's car, and the woman starts the ignition. "Here we go" she chimes, as Pete rubs the frosty window of the passenger seat. Looking out the window, the boy looks at the falling snow-flakes falling from the maroon sky.

"It looks a lot darker than it normally is" Pete observes. "It sure is. I wonder why?" April replies, to her son, as the car drove down the icy December road. After about twenty minutes, the two of them park alongside a crowded market, filled with various vendors.

"What are you going to have, Pete? Do you have a favorite thing to eat here?" his mother asks, as she sets the automobile's shift stick into park. "Favorite? I dunno. It's all pretty good here" Pete tells her. Exiting and slamming the car doors shut, they step out, and begin to browse the selections the vendors offer. "Yeah, I know what you mean. I like it all, too. Hard to say, what I'll get" April says, as the décor of the marketplace catches the boy's eye.

"I've never seen Christmas decorations like that" Pete says, pointing to a Christmas tree near the concession stand. Taking a pair of glasses out of her coat, April puts them on, as the two of them look up at the massive tree.

"Are those supposed to be little Dracula's heads?" the woman remarks, of the ceramic ornaments hanging from the tree's branches. "I think so. That's weird to see around this time of year. It's kinda like they've combined Halloween and Christmas, together" Pete says. The faces on the ornaments, appear to be hand crafted, with dark red eyes, and pointed little fangs, in their mouths.

"Is all the food here Romanian?" Pete asks as he and his mother order their dishes from the stand. "Not all of it. But, a large portion of it is. It makes sense that they decided to move the castle here, doesn't it? Since the city usually has this market going during the season. That makes it perfect" she says, taking a bite into her ethnic street food.

"It sure has a lot of garlic" Pete says, coughing after having taken a bite into a meat roll. "Yeah, it's a staple of their cuisine" April tells her son. "Is that why all the vampire movies and stuff always have the vampires allergic to it?" Pete asks, wiping the food from his lips.

"I don't know. The food vendors here, would probably know though. The staff here, are all from Eastern Europe. I imagine a lot of them are from Romania. Maybe even Transylvania, itself" the woman answers. Walking back into their car, the two of them make their way to the parking garage near their destination.

"Wow, I can even see it all the way from back here" Pete says, looking at the castle as April drives her car into the garage. "I know, right? Imagine how much time it must've taken them all to move that thing here. Not to mention, the cost of it all" she says, stopping the car.

"It looks cool having a big old castle like that in the middle of the city. Seeing it so close to all the skyscrapers and other buildings looks so unique" Pete says, in observation. "Yeah, it sure does. Okay, let's go, Pete" she says parking into the oversized parking garage. "Okay, Mom" the boy says, opening the door, setting his feet outside.

"That was a long drive. I can't believe it took us nearly the whole afternoon to get downtown. I don't ever remember traffic being this bad, before" April remarks, as she and Pete step stood in the nearly empty lot. "Well, it is the holiday season, Mom. Most people are off, either from their classes or work. Shopping, and doing things with their families" Pete says to his mother.

"Right. Kind of like what you and I are doing, right now?" she says, looking at the boy cheerfully. "Speaking of which, why is it so empty here? I was worried we wouldn't manage to get a parking spot. We're practically the only ones here" April says, turning her head around the lot.

"Yeah, it is pretty empty. Who knows? It's probably like I said, everyone is just really busy doing other stuff. Maybe they're all out of state on vacations" Pete explains to his mother. "That's true, but that's also all the more reason why I speculated it might be packed, here. This city is a pretty big travel destination. A lot of people travel to Chicago in the winter" she answers the boy, as their voices echoes throughout the nearly vacant lot.

"Then again, I guess it's kind of unusual for a mother to bring her son to Dracula's Castle during the Christmas season. It's not the type of thing people do around this time, normally. But that's kind of nice, isn't it? Doing something different for a change?" she says, as Pete becomes even more disturbed by all the uncanny events.

"Sure, Mom" Pete replies. "This is just getting ridiculous now. Unless this is all some kind of elaborate prank, I'm not sure how all these coincidences are even possible. Besides, there's no way she could have read the story my friends and I had written. The boy reflects, as he thought back how the notes he had before, seldom left his backpack.

April shuffles through her coat pocket in front of their parked car muttering to herself. "What on Earth? I just locked the car, and I can't find my keys" she says in a panicked tone. "Ouch!", she shouts, as the woman pulls out a pair of scissors from her coat pocket. There's a small laceration across her index finger. She nurses the wound in her mouth. "Not again" she says, cursing under her breath. "How did this get in here? Where are my keys?" April says, baffled by the situation.

A jingling noise swept across the nearly empty parking garage, and whistles down their eardrums. Pete and his mother, turn around swiftly, startled by the noise. Across them in the parking garage, stood a figure wearing some sort of a long black cloak. "Is that...my keychain?" April says, in uneasy disbelief. The figure, obscured by the darkness, jingles the keys in its clutches. "Who are you!?" April shouts from across the lot.

"We've been expecting you two" the figure replies. Do I know you?" April asks again. Scared, Pete grasped his mother's coat, as she placed her hand on his shoulder. "It's a woman" Pete says, as the boy squints his eyes, looking at her from across the cold garage. It was difficult to make out her figure, due to the lighting, but he was able to discern that much. She sounded old. More than that. There was something off about the way she sounded. It was her eerie, ghostly tone of her voice. Something seemingly, supernatural.

The jingling noise, rang again, as the old woman slowly and steadily began walking toward the pair. The woman began laughing uncontrollably, her voice no longer in the calm low tone as before. "She's crazy" April whispered to Pete. Walking closer, the woman now stood fully visible, in the middle of the garage. She was an old woman, with dirty unkempt wild long hair, and a black cloak, which looked like something a monk would wear. It was at this moment, April realized she had seen the woman, before. The pushy woman, from her commute on the train, who insisted to April she should come visit the castle.

"What's going on here, Ma'am?" April asks, as she remembered the pair of scissors in her pocket. She didn't want to, but April realized that she could use it in self-defense, if this woman were to try to get violent with her and Pete. The enigmatic woman's full ghoulish appearance grows completely clear in the light. "She might not be anything otherworldly, but she could still be dangerous. Even an old woman could present a threat if they're mentally ill" Pete thought to himself as the old woman stepped closer to their parking spot.

"You came. I had a feeling you would. I'm so happy" the figure says drawing ever nearer to the frightened mother and son. Now that she was closer, Pete was able to see that she was clutching something in her hands. It indeed was his mother's car keys.

"How did you get those?" April asked her. "Would you like them back?" the old woman asks, as she lets out a ghostly giggle. "Yes. Now enough fooling around, please give me my car keys back, Miss." April demanded. "If this is a joke, it's gone a bit too far, now" Pete's mother said, in a scolding manner.

The woman laughed, as if she understood something, they're in the dark about. "Everyone is talking about your son, where I'm from" she remarked. "Where you're from?" April asks her, wondering how this woman could know Pete. April grabs Pete's hand, as they now began discretely backing away. "Where's security, when you need them? Are we the only ones down here in the parking garage with her?" Pete asked himself as cold beads of sweat began to drip down his forehead.

"Where I'm from? Well, the little club I'm part of has gone by many names. The Order of the Serpent, long ago back in Romania. The Thule

Society, back in Germany. Don't worry about your keys, Miss. You and your son are not going to need them. Not where you're going. You're not going home. Not tonight" the cloaked woman said, with dark conviction in her breath.

"I'm only going to ask you one last time. Who are you?!" April yelled. Pete and her, were now well aware this woman was nothing short of a threat, despite her frail appearance. The ghastly woman sneered. "Calm down. Come this way. Inside the castle" she says, pointing toward the parking garage's exist.

As the two of them already came there to visit the castle, they do as she says, while keeping their distance. "I'm going to get security, once I get there" April says sternly, as the cloaked woman continues her creepy chuckling. Swinging the door open, the mother and son walk through the exit and onto their final destination, at last.

Chapter 23: Dracula's Castle

"It looks just like in the old scary movies..." Pete said as he and his mother stood in front the behemoth of a castle. A snowstorm had started, as the cold December air blew harshly against their dry pale faces. "I should have dressed warmer" Pete remarks to his mother, as the boy placed his hands over his freezing cold ears. "I told you to wear a hat, didn't I?" April says to the boy.

"Here take mine, Pete" she says, as the woman removes her winter hat. "No way. That's a girl's hat" Pete protests. "That's just silly, Pete. That doesn't matter. Anyway, we're here. I'm sure it's warm inside" she says to her son, as the two of them enter the castle's tall magnificent jaw bridge.

Stepping inside, the two of them stomp their boots on the carpeted matted floor. The snow quickly melts off their boots, as the interior of the castle was heated by flames spouting atop bright gothic torches in the castle's entrance. A metallic clanging sound is heard, as the enormous jaw bridge the two had entered from begins to close. "It sounds like someone must know we're here, Mom" Pete says, as the passageway they had entered from had now been shut.

"Hello? Is anyone here!?" April shouts, as the two of them walk about the castle's front entrance. "Mom, what's that noise?" Pete asks her, as he looks toward the end of the foyer. "I think it's coming from over there" she says, as they look over to a flowing draped cloth, which seemed to be concealing whatever was making the faint sounds.

Gentle footsteps, and soft murmurs fill the castle, as a dozen people slowly emerge from it's corridors. Standing amongst Pete and his Mother, the two of them gasp when they notice the long dark garments they had on. "They're wearing the same thing that old lady had on" Pete worriedly whispers to his mother. "I know" April says, as she begins to tremble as the cloaked figures encircle the two.

"You're probably wondering what's going on. Please, allow me to explain" says a female member of the group, as they surround Pete and April. Their formation made the boy think it seemed as if they were forming a sinister circle of duck, duck, goose. "It's her, again" Pete says, as he looks at the cloaked woman. It was the same woman they had met in the parking garage.

Pointing at the center of her robe's hood, the woman asks, "Do you know what this emblem means?" Pete hadn't noticed it before, due to the distance between them in the lot. Now that he's standing closer, Pete was able to discern the appearance of the icon she pointed to on her black hood.

"Ouroboros" the words slip out Pete's mouth in astonishment. The same drawing of the serpent eating its own tail, that he had depicted in his writing. Nearly identical from the illustration he had drawn on Halloween night. Except, this was not an amateurish drawing sketched by a child. This depiction looked more like an engraving. She and the other members of whatever it was they were part of, donned the same icon on the hood of each one of their robes.

"Yes, that's correct. The logo used in the past by the groups I mentioned before. The Order of the Serpent, The Thule Society. It's ours, too. Although the names may have changed in the past, our organizations are all one in the same. We change names throughout the ages, to remain concealed from the common man. Even Count Dracula himself, and Heinrich Himmler had robes just like these. Many many years ago.

"What the hell are you talking about?" April asks, in both terror and intrigue. "The people I just mentioned? Why they were very dedicated members to our cause" the cloaked woman responds. "Cause? What cause?" Pete inquires, of the mysterious lady.

"Our organization deals with the practice of magic. The science behind one's own will. The practice of focusing one's thoughts, or prayers if you prefer that term. The belief that mankind can essentially generate results into reality, if enough people want something enough. Prayers, but to a much more extreme degree" the darkly cloaked woman explains to them.

"Do you know who Heinrich Himmler was? He was Adolf Hitler's right hand man, in World War II. It's widely known that he was deep into occult practices, and ours is the same group he was part of. It was called The Thule Society in his time. Before him, The Order of the Serpent in Dracula's time, when he had membership in it. We mean to bring about a new world order, by willing a being capable of tremendous destruction into it" she continues.

"A Being?" April asks, scratching her chin with her still bleeding finger. "There are already so many legends based on Count Dracula, and we thought maybe we could take advantage of that. Sure, he might not have actually been a vampire or anything like that. Since vampires don't really exist. But, if we capitalize on the imagination of all of those who are intrigued by legends such as that, perhaps we can morph something like that into the real world" the woman, explains.

It's said that's what Himmler was trying to do back then, with some kind of destroyer deity. It doesn't even matter if our members believe in whatever we're trying to create. Only that if enough people concentrate on the same thing and will it into reality. Whether it existed or not, yet. Then, make it do their bidding. Problem is, we need a lot of people, to pull something of such a large scale off."

"That's absolutely nuts" April, mocks the

woman's idea. "Is it? I'm basically talking about a being retroactively creating itself, in a sense. If it's truly that great, it's power is worthy of worship isn't it? Besides, I don't think your son would find it too far off from what he already tested" the cloaked woman says. "We sensed your son's talent, from a game he played with his friends which successfully managed to provide similar results. They managed to conjure up something, and we believe he could be an invaluable asset to our organization. He popped up on our radar once he did that. You don't just pull off something like that without us noticing, and we've had our eyes set on him, ever since" she retorts, looking Pete straight in his green eyes.

"I-It wasn't successful" Pete says, hesitantly. "You don't remember do you? That's because when the event ended for you, it took your memories of the occurrence with it. Hints and reminders every now and then, may slip into your reality, afterward. Surely you must've noticed some happening? If you had more people involved, it would remain in your world, and wouldn't have to go" she tells the boy.

Pete pauses. He couldn't refute her words. As fantastical as it seemed, her explanation was beginning to make sense to the boy. "You remember the broadcast you watched the other day? Look over there" the woman says pointing to one of the members next to her. Another figure, donning the same black robe, removes it's hood. It was a man who Pete thought he had seen somewhere. After a moment or two, the young man realized it was the news reporter they had seen on TV from yesterday.

"That broadcast was beamed exclusively at your home, to get your attention. We're glad you saw it. This man's true loyalty is with us, with our organization. What you saw, wasn't even from an actual news station, as it was filmed here, with our resources. A facade, as is the reason why we brought Dracula's Castle here to create it for the resort. It's sort of a front, for our actual desires. We needed some way to generate revenue for our society, and this seemed like a good way to do so. That way, we can continue to thrive in secrecy, and provide funds for our goals."

"We've already accomplished that much. We've generated more than enough money through this, by means of publicity, alone. The castle we're in now, is going to serve as the catalyst to trigger everything" the woman explains.

"Why do you need me?" Pete inquires. Walking toward the young man, the ghostly woman pulls out a sheet of paper from a pocket in her cloak. "We're recruiting people who have an aptitude for creative writing. Surely you must recognize at least a few of the faces on that list" the woman in the robe, says to him with certainty. The boy's jaw dropped, as Pete held the sheet close to his face. "Yes. I know who some of them are" he says softly.

On the sheet of paper, there was a famous horror author who Pete knew of. Most people, in the world, probably did. The man had written many books spanning back several decades. Next to his photo, was a woman. Another world famous novelist known for writing fantasy novels. On the bottom of the list of faces, was a picture of himself. Pete.

"We're going to use their writing prowess to generate even richer tales, about the beast we're attempting to create. They're already popular, and if we can siphon enough of the collective focus of their readers imaginations, we can use it to generate the results we want. That is, after we trigger the event's catalyst, I mentioned" she continues.

"What do you mean by catalyst?" Pete asks of his shadowy hostess. "You know how ancient civilizations used to make sacrifices to their gods? It's the same principle. Mass human sacrifices were preformed while pyramid's were constructed ages ago, and we're going to do the exact same thing here" the woman tells the young man.

"Even Count Dracula himself did just that, before. Did you know that? In his time in Transylvania, he proclaimed to his community that he was going to solve the homeless problem, in his region in Eastern Europe. Naturally, the homeless members in his Transylvanian town were elated, and the Count arranged to have a feast for all of them in a wing of his castle."

"Count Dracula, then locked and burned the dining hall they were in, down to the ground. That was his inventive solution of solving the homeless problem. Just one of the many mass sacrifices the man participated in. The slaughter of the homeless people, his forest of dead corpses. He wasn't called Vlad the Impaler for nothing"

"We're going to do the exact same thing, on a much larger scale with this castle. An offer of extreme desolation, for our deity. Once it's up and running, we're going to burn the castle to the ground. We've already made all the necessary preparations. The castle was reconstructed with extremely flammable materials, which will make the fire spread so fast, it will burn down before help can ever arrive. On paper, it'll just look like corners were cut, in order to construct the building as cheaply as possible."

"Nobody will question it, and then we can move onto the next step, of reshaping the world, with the help of the greatest authors in modern memory" she tells them. "You mean the two people on this list? Wait, these people, agreed to help you?" Pete asks the old woman. Smirking the darkly cloaked woman walks over to a large draped cloth toward the end of the castle's foyer. "Why don't you ask them, yourself?" she says, in a humorous sounding tone.

Extending her arm, the woman takes her hand

216

and pulls down the curtain. Now uncovered, were the two authors Pete had recognized from the list. There they sat helpless, with their arms and legs tied with ropes to a pair of chairs. Duct-tape remained stretched across their mouths, as their eyes looked at Pete in fear.

"Will you be the first one to decide to join us?" the sinister woman asks, awaiting his answer. "This is despicable. Wanting my son to join your crazy cult? It's said that Hell is the fate of those who cause a child to sin. Besides, your plan is asinine. It's contrived and won't work " April tells the evil woman. Not knowing what to say, silence filled the castle, as the boy realized this wasn't a situation he could just walk away from. The way he saw it he had two choices. Either join this absurd and criminal cult or become one of their victims.

"Is that your, answer Pete? Rejection?" the woman asks, as she slowly walks around the boy, as if a cat stalking it's prey. "Mom, run!" Pete says, as he decides to take the offensive. "What are you doing?" the evil woman says, as Pete quickly rushes toward the cold stone wall of the castle.

"Stop him!" the mad woman shouts, as she sees the boy grab one of the tourches heating the room. Taking it off the wall, the young man thrusts the blazing torch atop the draping which had previously been thrown onto the floor, as the fire quickly began to engulf it.

Shocked by the child's resourceful spontaneity, the other members of the cult jolt back, feeling the heat of the flames in their faces. "No, you idiot! Are you trying to kill yourself, too?" the woman screams, reaching out for the boy. Defending her son, April pulls the pair of scissors out of her pocket and thrusts it toward the vixen.

Blood oozes out of the upper abdomen of the wicked mistress, as April holds the bloodied pair of scissors in her hand. In shock and anguish, the sinister woman screams. Falling to her knees the burning drape, catches the bottom of her coat. Taken off guard, the rest of the cult begin to take a tactical retreat. The cloaked members move quickly toward a marble door and run inside it.

"Get in quick! We'll get out through here!" the man Pete had seen on the television says to the woman, as they pull off her burning robe. Uncloaked and burned, two of the members hold her up with their shoulders as the others begin to close the door. "If the boy won't join us, we can let him burn down with the castle" the vicious woman says, with spit flying out of her mouth, like a rabid mad dog.

Slamming the door shut, the cult escapes through their secret passageway, hoping to seal Pete and April's fate amongst the inferno. "I got them untied!" April exclaims, clipping the tied ropes off of the hostages. Pete, his mother, and their two rescuee's, swiftly run toward the castle's labyrinthian set of corridors, as the blazing flames continue to spread along the castle walls.

"How are we supposed to know how to get out of here?" Pete shouts, as the quartet peers down one of the dimly lit corridors. Standing at the front, Pete's green eyes move side to side, investigating the labyrinth, with what little light remained within it. "Go this way, Pete" an echoing voice whispers to the boy.

"Mom, did you hear that?" Pete says, wondering where the voice had come from. It had sounded familiar to the boy. "Hear what? I didn't hear anything. "Let's try this way" Pete commands, as the the four of them head in the direction the voice had suggested. Speedily, they lunge forward and embark down the hallway. "I think I can see some light", Pete says as his eyes squint. It's nearly pitch black, but the spreading flames along with the tourches on the wall, illuminate the hallway.

"You're almost out. Keep going" the mysterious voice says to the boy, continuing to provide advice. "That voice..." While franticly running, Pete thought to where he remembered the voice. An old memory flashed in his mind. It was the same voice he had remembered before, from Halloween night, back when he thought of his father reading The Velveteen Rabbit to him, as an infant.

"That sounded like...Dad?" Pete thought, as they continued their escape. His father had died when he was just a baby. Pete barely remembered anything about his dad, since he was so young. One of the things the boy did remember fairly well, was his voice. The voice he had heard, did indeed sound like how his father had sounded in his memories. No, not Joe the fictional man he had written in his story, but rather his actual father, who had died before he ever had the opportunity to get to know the man.

Approaching the exit, the visage of an enormous apparition begins to materialize in front of the four, as if trying to prevent their escape from the burning castle. It had a human form yet furrowed it's brow in an angry reptilian like scowl. It screams in haste, as it reaches for the boy with long clawed clutches. Phasing through Pete, its attempted attack, had no effect. The being lets out a furious roar, as they continue toward the light glistening out of the exit.

"Have to keep going" the young man muttered, nearly out of breath. His head shuffles surveying the darkness. "Yes...there's the exit" Pete whispers through his lips, as the four of them reach an opened door, and escape the depths of the castle's shadowy domain.

The lights of firetrucks approach the four, as they look back up at the burning castle. Having arrived too late, the firemen watch with Pete, his mother and the two authors, as the castle collapses into a conflagration of scorching hot flames. Just as how the Velveteen Rabbit, had been swallowed by the flames in the fairy tale, the castle burned to ash, just the same. Pete hoped the same applied to the monstrous figure he had seen in it, just before his escape. The sirens of the trucks stop, and taking their place was the sound of church bells, tolling in the distance.

"Looks like it's Christmas, now" April says, as a fireman approaches the pair. "Are you two, okay?" the man asks, handing them some blankets to provide warmth on the cold night. "Yes, I'm fine. How about you, Pete?" She turns, as the boy covers himself with the warm cloth. "Yeah, Mom" he answers her, as they continue to watch the wretched castle burn away, into the dark of the night.

Chapter 24: Horror's End

Now back at home and unable to sleep, April and her son Pete, sit quietly in their living room. April sips a cup of tea, while watching the television, while the young man sits on the couch reading a book. "How about turning off the news, Mom? I think we've both heard enough about that for the day" Pete suggests, as he notices that the program on the television had shifted to a report about the castle's fire.

"Yeah, you can say that again. You acted bravely tonight, Pete. I'm proud of you. I think your dad would be, too" she tells her son. "I have a feeling he was with us tonight" Pete says, as he closes the page of the book he's reading. "You're not still reading Dracula, are you?" April asks the boy as she sits up out of her chair. "No, I'm reading something else" he tells her.

April walks over to her son and looks at the book's cover. "Oh my. That's a story I don't think I've heard in a long time" his mother comments. Pete nods his head. "Me too."

Horror's Call

A series of interconnected horror novels that can be read in any order. Each book serves as a stand alone story, yet builds a greater picture behind a dark mystery in Chicago.

Call of the Crocodile

A dark fantasy horror novel, set during Halloween. After a boy is eaten alive by a crocodile, his family begins a descent into madness and terror in this odyssey of modern horror.

Call of the Kappa

After a mysterious visitor stops by his martial arts gym, Arnold begins to suspect there's something supernatural about the stranger. Set in July, Call of the Kappa is a horror novel, which is filled with the spirit of the season. Independence Day, and of the terror about to strike.

Call of the Arcade

A sci-fi horror novel about the most mysterious arcade game ever made. Two friends travel to an arcade in downtown Chicago, which they suspect may contain a haunted arcade machine from urban legends- Polybius. Unknown horrors await them, as they inch ever closer to the truth behind the sinister arcade game.

Call of the Cherokee

A horror/mystery saga into the depths of a haunted theater! Recently reconstructed, the formerly burned down Cherokee Theater is once again open for business. After receiving an invitation, three friends decide to check out the theater, curious as to what all the hype's been about.

Call of the Cradle

A single young mother and her son are stalked by a ghostly menace in Chicago. A monster, responsible for unspeakable acts, not limited to this world. Set in the aftermath of September 11th, the city of Chicago feels a sense of impending danger, fearing a similar tragedy could occur. A fast paced horror odyssey, which all begins on Halloween.